As the biggest tear-gem of the Great Spirit streaked through the forge's open window and fell onto the hilt of the sacred sword, all the blacksmiths stopped, amazed. The sword was finished! Pepheroh touched the perfect blade with a claw. "I shall save you for the hero," he vowed.

Seasons passed. In a holy chamber, the sword lay in a crystal case, waiting for its master to come.

ALSO BY NANCY YI FAN:

SWORDBIRD

SWORD QUEST

NANCY YI FAN

ILLUSTRATIONS BY
JO-ANNE RIOUX

HarperTrophy®
An Imprint of HarperCollinsPublishers

Sword Quest

Text copyright © 2008 by Nancy Yi Fan

Illustrations copyright © 2008 by Jo-Anne Rioux

www.harpercollinschildrens.com

Library of Congress Cataloging-in-Publication Data
Fan, Nancy Yi.
    Sword quest / Nancy Yi Fan. — 1st ed.
        p.   cm.
    Summary: Wind-voice, a dove, seeks a sword made magical by
the Great Spirit himself in order to save the world of birds from
destroying themselves at war, but first he must confront an evil
rival, archaeopteryx Maldeor.
    ISBN 978-0-06-124337-0
    1. Children's writings, American. [1. Birds—Fiction. 2.
Archaeopteryx—Fiction. 3. Dinosaurs—Fiction. 4. War—Fiction.
5. Fantasy. 6. Children's writings.] I. Title.
PZ7.F19876Swm 2008   2007041936
[Fic]—dc22   ·   CIP
                                              AC

Typography by Amy Ryan
❖
First Harper Trophy edition, 2009

TO ALL WHO WANT TO BE
MASTERS OF FATE

TABLE OF CONTENTS

The World of Birds

PERIDOT RIVER

WHITE CAP
MOUNTAINS

ROCKWELL RIVER

Augoric
Ocean

KAURIA, THE ISLAND
OF PARADISE

LANDS AND TERRITORIES CLAIMED
BY ARCHAEOPTERYXES AND THEIR
ALLIES

LEASORN GEM

WIND-VOICE'S PATH

WIND-VOICE AND STORMAC'S PATH

EWINGERALE AND FLEYDUR'S PATH

MALDEOR'S PATH

This is a special sword,
a sword that can change the world.
—FROM THE OLD SCRIPTURE

A Sword Is Made

Rosy clouds of dawn floated over the Island of Paradise. King Pepheroh of Kauria crouched among the fronds of the tallest palm tree, his linen robe and tail feathers whipping in the breeze. The old phoenix meditated on the Great Spirit with his eyes half open, hoping to hear his will, but his mind was distracted by the troubling news his messengers had been bringing him for many months.

Between the earth and the sky, birds were struggling. Once they had freely shared trees and nest space, seeds, roots, and berries, but, somehow, arguments had arisen. That led to cheating, then to stealing, and then to pecking and scratching. As time rolled steadily on, the most powerful winged creatures, feuding with one another, had turned to weapons. Four-winged dinosaurs and archaeopteryxes swooped down, killing and destroying. War spread across the ptero-world like a hurricane so that now nearly all lived in fear, distrust, and uncertainty. Pepheroh's magical kingdom was one of the last peaceful lands remaining.

"Help us, Great Spirit," Pepheroh cried. "Send us a sign."

A sound came drifting on the wind, so faint that Pepheroh at first thought it was only his own hope whispering in his ear. But then he heard it again.

Make a sword, the Great Spirit told him. *Somebird has to guide the world into order again. Make a sword, and he will come to wield it.*

Can a sword truly be used to bring peace to the world? Pepheroh wondered as he clutched his garments around him. "How can I forge such a powerful sword?"

When the sword is nearly finished, I shall make it magical. But beware, the Great Spirit warned. *Guard the sword until a worthy bird comes to claim it on the day of the fifth full moon three years from now. If an evil bird wields it, it will bring more disaster to the world.*

"Yes, Great Spirit," Pepheroh promised.

After the blacksmiths and metalworkers all over Kauria heard the old king's proclamation, they came to present their service and skills.

A month passed. Pepheroh was visiting the forge at dusk. *Will this sword be a blessing or a curse?* he thought anxiously as his eyes followed every stroke of the hammer.

Suddenly, Pepheroh saw a flash of light beaming down from the sky. He realized that it was the tear of the Great Spirit, who was saddened at the warring world. The glistening drop fell onto the earth and shattered into eight gemstones, the largest bearing all the colors of the rainbow, and each of the others glistening with one of its colors.

As the biggest tear-gem of the Great Spirit streaked through the forge's open window and fell onto the hilt of the sacred sword, all the blacksmiths stopped, amazed. The sword was finished! Pepheroh touched the perfect blade with a claw. "I shall save you for the hero," he vowed.

Seasons passed. In a holy chamber, the sword lay in a crystal case, waiting for its master to come.

Not all was well in Kauria. The dark power of chaos began to reach toward the island like a devil bird's claws, and the island's green lushness started to fade away.

"Will a hero come?" the old king asked.

"Your Highness, I will go out to find him!" Ozzan the toucan blacksmith said. "I have seen scores of years, and my life's work was the hero's sword. It is my wish to see

it wielded by the right bird, so I will go out into the mortal world and find this hero."

"But Ozzan, it is dangerous for you." Pepheroh reached out a claw to place a magical protection, but the toucan stopped him.

"Keep your strength for the protection of our island,

my good king. This decision is my own," he said, and flexed a claw to prove his strength. Under the worn, wrinkled skin there were still muscles from his younger days. "I will take a badge to remind me of my home and of you. I will see to it that a worthy bird comes."

There was a pause, and they could hear the wind blowing the sand around them. The toucan's blue-lidded eyes were shining.

"Very well, Ozzan. You may go."

Who loses and who gains
is settled within a flap of the wings.
—FROM THE OLD SCRIPTURE

1
LOSS

Hungrias II, the Ancient Wing, emperor of the archaeopteryxes, sprawled like a huge spider on his whalebone perch. He was staring out of a rounded window at the forests of Castlewood, but his eyes reflected the world. "Secrets. Delicious!" he declared, his bloated face squished into furrows. "No secrets can sneak past my mighty empire's eyes and ears. Yes, go on!" Down the great golden hall of the Sun

Palace, the rows of plumes on the leather headgear of his knights all dipped forward as the subjects leaned in to listen. Across from them, his scholars swished their sleeves.

"The lowly birds in your territories are starting to whisper about rare gemstones. Leasorn gems, they're called," the head of the scholars said. "They have strange markings on them. It is said they come from the sky and have something to do with a hero. One in particular, our sources reveal, seems to hint at when the hero will come—sometime in three years." The members of the court gasped. The scholar spread the claws of one foot wide in wonderment, then closed them abruptly. He pointed at a ragamuffin twitching beside him. "I have found a witness, Your Majesty!"

"Speak."

"Yes, Your Majesty!" the young archaeopteryx said. "I chanced to see that particular stone during my morning foraging. 'Thank the Great Spirit the gem is here,' one of the birds around it was saying, so I knew something was peculiar. I hid and watched . . ."

Magical stones from the sky! thought the emperor, his gaze sweeping across the sunset painted on the arched ceiling.

"Color! Location! Tribe!" Hungrias's eyes glittered as

if two gemstones were already in his pupils. "Speak up!"

"Beautifully orange it was, Your Majesty. It's about a couple dozen miles south of your Plains territory, with a band of doves living near a river."

Sounds like something for me. Hero, the wise bird said? Well, I'll show how archaeopteryxes can crush all heroes! "I must have this treasure." Drumming his sausagelike talons, Hungrias straightened on his jeweled perch and barked, "Sir Maldeor!"

"Yes, Your Majesty." The head of the knights stepped forward on the carpet and bowed.

"Take some elite soldiers and find this gem for me."

Before the knight could reply, the curtains behind Hungrias's throne trembled and a fat feathered ball waddled up to the emperor. "Me too!" Prince Phaëthon cried, his beak full. In his claws he held a blueberry muffin. "I shall go along. I must!"

"You're young. Battles are not for you."

"I must! I want to learn how to fight. Please, Father!" the prince begged, crumbs on his beak.

Hungrias's tiny eyes flitted shut. Then he huffed and said, "Sir Maldeor, I entrust my son to you."

Phaëthon grinned with green-tinged teeth.

Good grief, thought the knight. "Yes, Your Majesty," he managed to say.

The next day, Sir Maldeor, Prince Phaëthon, and thirty soldiers journeyed to the dove tribe.

Easy picking, Maldeor thought when they arrived. The squat, knobbly olive trees where the tribe lived did not seem to present a threat, but because of the prince, precautions had to be taken. "Stay behind the first line," Maldeor whispered.

"Why? I hate that!" shouted the prince, surprising a dove named Irene coming back from a morning flight. She rushed toward her tribe, shouting, "Archae-opteryxes! They're coming, they're coming!"

Surprise plan foiled! Maldeor spat in disgust and flipped his long tail to signal the charge. As if that weren't enough, as the soft fluttering wings of the defending doves obscured the olive trees beyond, Phaëthon whined in the knight's ear, "Can I find the gem?"

"No, Prince. Not now."

Why did the prince want to come in the first place? I can't be a nursemaid and a knight at the same time, Maldeor thought as he muttered plans to a group of his soldiers. With a nod, they formed into a tight ball prickling with spears and flew directly at the biggest olive tree. An old dove was frantically burying the gemstone in a hollow of the tree. Beside him stood Irene, the bird who had forewarned their tribe.

The knight aimed for the Leasorn gem, but the old dove jumped and kicked Maldeor's face with his pink claws. Maldeor bit one toe and hung on. The old dove tried to beat Maldeor off, but he was too small to have much chance. One of Maldeor's soldiers swung a club.

"Flee, my daughter!" the old dove gasped, and died.

"No!" Irene shrieked. Sobbing, she tensed her neck and, with a mighty flap of her wings, dived at Maldeor's claws, which now held the gemstone. Maldeor whooped in pain. The stone sailed out of his grip, out of the olive tree, and landed a way off, in a sandy ditch. With grunts and *Yahh!*s, the birds propelled themselves madly toward it. Maldeor forgot the dove and scrambled to see. He sighed in relief when he saw that an archaeopteryx reached the gem first. "Yes!"

But it was none other than the prince. Turning in the direction of Maldeor, he lifted the gem up in the air. "*I have found the gem!*" Phaëthon pronounced, gloating.

You little bother! Maldeor grumbled angrily to himself and gripped his sword tighter. He gave a curt order to his soldiers to kill all the doves they could find. The foolish birds would have to pay for their defiance of the emperor—and Maldeor would have to go and get the prince. If only he hadn't agreed to bring the brat here. As if in answer to his hidden wishes, a dark shadow suddenly loomed from the grove of birches behind the prince.

Now, this was no dove or archaeopteryx. It was the last of the long-lived flying creatures who had four wings. This intelligent creature, neither reptile nor bird, had blundered along in the darkness of the bracken for years and years and years, revealing himself to his contemporary cousins only when necessity called. Lizard eyes staring, he scanned the battleground he had just come across and focused on a young, tender specimen. *A bigger bite than the doves,* he thought. The evil cogwheels in his ancient brain whirled as he calculated.

He sprang into the sunlight, unfurling four wings. For trembling seconds the dinosaur eclipsed the sun, then, lifting its leathery lips, bore down on the fat young prince.

The mouth opened, in went the front half of the prince, and the mouth closed. The prince's muffled squeals came echoing out of the creature's nostrils. Six times the size of an archaeopteryx, the monster jerked its neck, trying to swallow.

"Prince, Prince!" Sir Maldeor yelled hoarsely, grudges forgotten, as pure fear flooded his being. What was this? Was the prince dead already? *My knighthood and life are in jeopardy!* He jumped toward the four-winged dinosaur. His soldiers swarmed to corner the new danger as well, but their spears clattered off its scales and did not worry it. Now the fat legs and tail of the prince were kicking between the teeth. Maldeor grabbed one round leg and started desperately pulling.

Phaëthon, in the throat of the monster, was suffocating. *He has little hope,* Maldeor thought, and tugged at the gemstone instead. He wrestled fiercely to uncurl the stiffening talons, even beating on the prince's foot with his sword, but it seemed of little use. Like any dying bird, the prince's claws fastened tightly to whatever he was holding in an iron clutch.

Maldeor succeeded in loosening two toes, but just as the gemstone wobbled, the dinosaur broke loose, reared on its hind legs, and tipped its head back. Phaëthon disappeared, gem and all.

Before Maldeor could try to slash open the creature's throat and belly to retrieve the prince's body and get the gemstone, a sudden deep groan issued from the winged monster. Its eyes shriveled up like two huge raisins, and, with a horrified bellow, it dropped to all fours and disappeared in a wreath of blue flames.

Sir Maldeor hacked the air as fiercely as he could where the monster had been, but it was gone, along with the prince and the gemstone. He looked back in despair. The dove who had knocked the gem out of his claws was nowhere to be seen. He howled in frustration and panic.

Meanwhile, Irene the dove mourned for her destroyed tribe and her dead father. Between each trembling wing beat, she distractedly wondered where she should head. An image of foaming waves flitted across her mind. The archaeopteryxes never patrolled the southern seaside, except on a rare mission. *Yes, the seaside would be a safe place to go for now,* she thought.

The trip that she made to the sea was an extraordinary one. Where it might have taken a seasoned migratory bird two days, she got there in just one day. Exhausted, she fell into a deep slumber in a crevice within a seaside cliff and did not wake till morning.

She felt wretched with despair. Now she had lost everything. Family, safety, responsibility. She staggered along the sand in the whispering tide, her vision blinding white with sickening grayish shadows.

A few days later, she laid an egg, and her interest in life was renewed. *I won't lose you to the archaeopteryxes, my little one,* she vowed. *I will die for you if I have to.*

The days that she brooded her egg brought the worst sea storms ever imagined. The clouds finally cleared on the day the egg trembled and broke; and a thread of light fell upon the small bird, who was covered with down as delicate as frost.

Irene stared at the hatchling, amazed. Doves never hatched with feathers! The strange little bird turned his face to his mother, and his eyes opened, dark and shining. But baby doves were hatched blind. In the distance the sea wind sang. Winds could be gentle or powerful. Winds could be captured, but never for long. Irene cupped her claw around her hatchling's head and whispered, "Wind-voice . . ."

Still, the hatchling looked a lot like her: red beak, red feet, and an honest little face with a perpetual smile on it. She feared, sadly and bitterly, that somehow the archaeopteryxes would be a threat to her hatchling.

When the four-winged dinosaur awoke in a room with shadowy granite walls, he was diminished in size. He pressed a trembling forelimb to his heart. Nothing was beating.

Before him, misty smoke whirled in a gigantic circle. High up in the very middle of the spinning gray wisps, a voice boomed out. "I am Yama, Lord of Death. Welcome, four-winged creature. You are no longer truly alive, but partially a ghost, and here you shall be known as Yin Soul. You have swallowed a sacred gemstone, a crystallized tear of my opposite, the Great Spirit. It is lodged inside you. This is your punishment! You shall be suspended here in torment in this small space, between the world of the living and the dead."

The dinosaur widened his eyes. "What? There must be a mistake! I didn't eat a gem; I ate an archaeopteryx!"

"The archaeopteryx was holding on to a gemstone. It is one of seven that points the way to the magical sword in Kauria, the Island of Paradise. A hero will come to get the sword in the fifth full moon two years from now. When he does, you shall die an utterly painful death."

Yin Soul yelped. "Can I get out? I don't want to be here!"

"Only if you manage to reincarnate in the body of a likely hero before Hero's Day and get the sword yourself will you escape. Otherwise, my realm shall welcome you!" Yama's voice sent chills through the dinosaur.

In the same mysterious way he had come, Yama dissolved.

There were bookshelves full of dark tomes all around Yin Soul. In the long, agonizing days after his arrival, he devoted himself to learning ways of trickery and deceit. All the while, he scanned the frozen thoughts of dying birds, searching—searching for a victim to pull him out of this wretched place.

He waited bitterly for two years before he finally found one.

Resistance is hatched from oppression.
—from the Old Scripture

2
THE DEFIANCE

No empire since the creation of the sword had spread so quickly or so ruthlessly as that of the archaeopteryxes. They were a shrewd, hardy species. The key to their sudden expansion was that they thrived on everything: fruit, seeds, insects, fish, and carrion. Soon most of the other tribes were serving them as slaves or paying them tribute. Even the powerful alliance of the crow, myna, and raven clans had fallen.

Some surrendered and, in return for their lives, agreed to serve in the archaeopteryx army. Only the eagles, in their remote mountain stronghold, lived free, but they were too busy guarding their own liberty to come to the aid of others.

The archaeopteryx empire was divided into six regions: Castlewood, or the Emperor's Wood; the Forests; the Dryland; the Plains; the Isles; and the Marshes. Each region was ruled by one of the emperor's most trusted officers. Sir Kawaka commanded the Marshes Battalion.

Early in the morning on the first day of winter, Kawaka was hosting a dinner for his officers, proudly displaying the treasures he had gathered for the Ancient Wing. A beautiful yellow crystal was his most magnificent tribute. He'd seized it from a tribe of weak little kingfishers only the week before. Wouldn't the emperor be pleased!

"To Sir Kawaka! To Emperor Hungrias! To the expansion of archaeopteryx territory!" The traditional toast rang from the leafless branches of the tree that Kawaka had made into his headquarters.

Below, in a storeroom hollowed out beneath the roots of the tree, a scrawny bird was scrubbing pots. His white feathers were smeared with grime, his red bill and feet blackened by grease. A dark smudge on his face almost covered the slash of red dye that marked him as a slave.

A bored sentry at the mouth of the cave sighed as he lit his pipe. Dubto could hear the toasts and the shouting from the branches above, but he was stuck here guarding this. *What kind of bird was that slave anyway?* Dubto thought. He looked like a dove but was bigger than any dove Dubto had ever seen. He supposed that was why they called the bird "013-Unidentified."

"Who're your parents?" he barked, blowing smoke rings out of his nostrils.

"My mother's a dove, but I've never seen my father," the young bird said. His voice was so weak that it was hard to hear above the sloshing of the pans.

So why did a feeble young drudge like this need his own guard? The fledgling barely looked strong enough to attack a greasy pot. Indeed, as the archaeopteryx watched, the white bird slumped over the cauldron he was scrubbing, too exhausted to continue.

"Here, you," Dubto said gruffly, and tapped his pipe. He didn't dare risk being seen or heard speaking to a slave with kindness in his voice. "Leave that. I need you to run an errand."

There was nothing truly urgent that needed to be done. But the slave would surely be the better for some fresh air.

"Yes, sir?" 013-Unidentified said weakly.

Dubto looked around and spotted a small barrel of ale, half hidden under a tree root. "Take that over to the outpost on the edge of camp," he said. "The sentry needs supplies."

Take your time, he almost added, but he thought he had been kind enough for one day. After all, the bird was a slave, not an archaeopteryx.

Outside, 013-Unidentified gulped in life-giving air, feeling the tiredness wash out of his sore back. His soul was dazzled by the azure spread that was the sky. He tried to fly, but the heavy cask of ale kept making him tip forward. He was outside! For months now, ever since he'd been captured by an archaeopteryx patrol, he'd been cooped up in the back of that earthen cave, alternately cleaning whatever pots and pans were flung at him and sleeping. He scanned the green-tinted ponds and the cedars looming nearby. *Howling winds!* he thought. *What a murky, frightening land!*

"Over here! The sun's barely up and I'm cold," a raucous voice rang out.

013-Unidentified handed over the cask of ale to the sentry, who was perched on the bare, gray limb of a dead tree near the entrance to a burrow in the ground. A clattering came from within the dark hollow.

The sentry popped the cork off the cask of ale and took a long drink while 013-Unidentified cocked his head to catch the sound. Then there was a muffled groan. "What is inside, sir?" he asked.

The sentry sighed in disgust. "Tomorrow's dinner, fool! Go back to your cave immediately, hear?" He jumped from his perch and glided toward 013-Unidentified.

013-Unidentified fluttered back. "But sir, I . . ."

The archaeopteryx swung his lance at the white bird's

face. 013-Unidentified dodged it, ducking under a branch. The archaeopteryx swooped after him, but his tail, dragging behind him, struck a tree branch. His wings flapped frantically and a strangled croak burst out. He dropped his lance, which barely missed 013-Unidentified.

Alarmed, 013-Unidentified stumbled backward. What was happening? Then he saw that a metal chain necklace around the archaeopteryx's neck had gotten caught. The sentry was choking and twisting. His necklace snapped. With a splash, he crashed into a puddle on the ground below.

013-Unidentified peered at him suspiciously, but the archaeopteryx didn't stir. A faint moan from inside the burrow made him remember what he had been curious about originally. He wasn't likely to have such a chance again; the archaeopteryxes usually watched him very closely. Cautiously he pushed aside some ferns at the entrance and ducked inside.

There was a flash of something moving behind some metal crates. 013-Unidentified took a few steps forward.

"Hello," he whispered into the darkness.

Something squirmed back away from him as far as it could.

"Who are you?" 013-Unidentified said under his breath. His eyes gradually adjusted to the dark and he could see the frail figure cowering inside one of the crates. A tattered vest covered black and white feathers; a red head gleamed in the murky darkness.

"Don't eat me . . ." The bird rested his head against the crate.

"*Eat* you?" 013-Unidentified gasped, horrified. He'd known for seasons now what the archaeopteryxes did with captives they thought too weak or too useless to make good slaves. But he'd never before had a chance to speak to what the sentry had called "tomorrow's dinner."

The next thing he knew he had picked up a rock and slammed it with all his might at the lock of the crate. He did not know how many times he repeated the action, but finally the lock gave way and he threw it aside with a sudden rush of fierce satisfaction. He leaned against the side of the burrow, gasping for breath, and said huskily, "Come out! Come out!"

The prisoner raised his tearstained eyes. "Thank you! I'm 216-Woodpecker." Then he added, "No, I'm Ewingerale . . . 'Winger.'"

"I am . . ." It had been so long since anybird had called the white bird by his true name that he found he had to grope in his memory for it. A scene flashed in his mind—his mother stroking his head tenderly, her sweet voice lingering in his ear. "I'm . . . Wind-voice."

Wind-voice hadn't planned to escape when he woke that morning. And when Dubto had ordered him outside, he hadn't planned to do anything more than stretch his wings. But now, with a broken lock, a freed prisoner, and an archaeopteryx lying unconscious in a puddle outside

the burrow, what choice did they both have but to fly as fast as they could?

"Now is the time to fly away," Wind-voice whispered.

"Let's go," Winger agreed.

From the corner of his crate Winger snatched up a quill and a piece of wood, which was carved in a peculiar curved shape, and followed Wind-voice outside. They both peered cautiously out of the entrance to the burrow. Nothing was to be seen. The puddle where the sentry had been lying was empty. Holding their breath, they stepped outside.

"Ha! You think you can just walk out?" From above them, the slime-covered sentry, recovered now, leaped down and crushed them with his claws.

Without thinking, Wind-voice twisted around and pecked madly at the face of the archaeopteryx guard. Not expecting such violence from a slave, the bird flinched, and Winger twisted free.

"Fly!" Wind-voice shouted. "Fly!"

"You filthy little slave!" the guard said, panting, and his claws gripped Wind-voice even more tightly as he made a second grab at the woodpecker.

Winger dodged, leaping into the air, but hesitated, hovering. "Fly!" Wind-voice cried. Winger swooped around, but helpless to do more, he took flight.

Wind-voice was no match for the stronger, heavier bird once the archaeopteryx had recovered from his surprise. In a moment he was pinned flat in the mud with the sentry's claws gripping his throat. The claws squeezed tighter and tighter. Darkness began to close in on Wind-voice's vision.

"Halt!"

The angry voice was faintly familiar to Wind-voice. The claws around his throat loosened, and he gasped for air. *Sir Kawaka*, he thought. Why was the commander of the Marshes Battalion intervening to stop the killing of a lowly slave?

"This one is not yours to punish, fool!"

Wind-voice wasn't sure what Kawaka meant by that, and nobird bothered to explain it to him as he was bound and forced back to his dark den under the roots of the headquarters tree. But even in that darkness, when he closed his eyes, he could almost see the woodpecker, with his bright red head, zipping away to freedom.

"Who let him out of the cave? Who?" Kawaka, garbed in silken tassels and gray-and-khaki uniform, shouted from a branch of his headquarters tree. Usually he only turned his profile to other birds, since his beak was slightly curved to one side in a way that looked half silly, half intimidating. "Crookbeak," the other knights called him behind his back. Lower-ranked birds didn't dare to talk about the beak, much less look at it. But now he was facing his soldiers, a bad sign.

The fifty or so officers in the Marshes Battalion stood at attention, eyes either looking off into space or focused strictly on the knight's forehead. Outside, lesser soldiers bustled about, sensing that something was wrong.

"I did, Kawaka, sir." The voice came from somewhere behind the barrel-chested local-resistance captains. "I was on maintenance duty."

"And you are?" Kawaka held his breath, trying not to shout at the fool.

"Dubto, spear-bird, of the sixth elite band of the tracking division of the Marshes Battalion."

Kawaka strode along the branch, trembling with impatience. "By my teeth! Do you know why I kept this mangy little crossbreed so carefully all these seasons? He could have been a nice dumpling in the supper pot!"

"Yes, sir," said Dubto mechanically. "You kept him to give to His Majesty the Ancient Wing. It is well known that the emperor likes rare gemstones and rare birds. But the fledgling was weakening, sir," Dubto said. "So I thought fresh air . . ."

"*Cheek!*" Kawaka screeched. He marched about

impatiently, the tassels on his chest fluttering with each huff of his breath.

A year before, while on a trip passing over the seaside, four of his soldiers had raided a cliff. After two of them had drawn away the mother and killed her, the remaining birds had seized her scrawny baby. Seeing its strangeness, they had reported it to Kawaka.

"All that work to keep him safe," Kawaka blustered, "and now this incident has sown seeds of rebellion in his heart. But time is running short! You," he ordered one of the birds, "put a heavy rope around 013-Unidentified's foot. We must start the journey." Kawaka snatched the yellow stone from its display stand and put it in a small wooden box. *At least I have this. The emperor will be pleased with me,* the knight thought.

Ewingerale bobbed up and down in his undulating flight. Alternating between mad bursts of wing flapping and short glides where he tucked in his wings, he paused only to pull up the hood of his tattered vest. His round red head was dangerously obvious in the woods.

But as the sun brightened, the hope that Wind-voice was still alive dimmed. The woodpecker's long tongue tensed in his skull and he swallowed hard. How could the white bird not have been sentenced to death already?

"Fate holds both grit and gold in store for us," he whispered to himself. If Wind-voice was fated to die, there was little that Winger could do to save him.

And yet, while languishing in that fetid cage, Winger had thought it must be his fate to perish, and Wind-voice had changed that. Maybe Wind-voice's fate could be changed as well. Winger knew he could not simply abandon his new friend, not after Wind-voice had saved his life. If there was any chance—the slightest ray of hope—that the strange white bird was still alive, Winger would peck and hammer with all his might, attempting a rescue.

I can't do it alone, but where in these hills and dales can I find help? he thought. He had been shipped here as a gift to Kawaka by a lesser official. That bird had thought the woodpecker's musical talents were something to enjoy, but clearly Kawaka had not agreed. The knight had ordered a guard to break all the strings on the woodpecker's harp and had tossed the prisoner into the back of the burrow.

A few days before, Kawaka had remembered him and decided he'd make a succulent meal. They'd tossed gigantic piles of potato peels into his cage hoping to fatten him up, but he had eaten none of it.

"Fate is good to me," he whispered to himself joyously,

for suddenly he spied a small wisp of smoke in the cedar groves north of the battalion camp. Perhaps some other birds lived nearby.

But then his head snapped back at the faint croaks of "Hey ho, hey ho!" behind him. Down he dropped, his heart pounding fearfully. From the thorns of a hawthorn tree, he glimpsed Kawaka flying purposefully in the lead of twenty or so birds, all laden down with odd packages. They were heading northwest.

His fears eased as he saw the archaeopteryxes streak past, not veering a feather from their straight path. The sight of white wings straggling behind an archaeopteryx made his neck prickle again. "Wind-voice is alive! Where are they going?"

Winger leaped out of hiding and bolted toward the line of smoke. An egret armed with darts splashed out from a pond and ordered him to stop. Winger obeyed, pouring out a jumble of words so quickly that the sentry could hardly understand.

"I'll take you to Fisher," the egret declared. "You can tell your tale to him."

Winger heard the camp before he saw it. The whetting of dozens of spearheads upon rock sounded like a brisk, deadly rain. Kingfishers, egrets, herons, and mynas bowed before their work. They seemed to be preparing for battle. Some practiced moves, jabbing with their spears, leaping back, and jabbing again in time with the grinding. Winger saw a great blue heron erect on a rock, and a stout myna leaning on his staff.

The heron had the air of a leader, so Winger darted to the bird, gasping out his story. "My friend, he saved me. He released me from the lair of the archaeopteryxes. But they caught him, they kept him, he couldn't—did you just see that train of birds? They were leading him away on a rope—"

The heron held up a wing and interrupted him. "A train of birds, you say? Were they carrying boxes and bundles?"

"Yes, yes!" Winger nodded eagerly. "And they are holding my friend captive. Please, can you—"

The heron looked down his long beak at the excited woodpecker. "My son, our goals are linked," he said. "Kawaka has stolen the amber stone of the kingfisher tribe. If what you say is true, he is bringing our stone as tribute to the Ancient Wing, the emperor of the archaeopteryxes. We have prepared for weeks, and we plan to attack them today. You must show us where they were flying. Perhaps we can rescue your friend as well as our gemstone."

Meanwhile, Kawaka winged on to meet his emperor. Hungrias had just arrived at his winter palace in the Marshes territory, where he went to escape the cold in the northern region of his empire, Castlewood.

"Hurry, hurry!" Kawaka called to his soldiers. He, as the regional knight, had to report to the emperor yearly with gifts and tributes. This year, twenty pack-soldiers accompanied him, some hanging onto barrels with hooked talons or clamped bills, others swinging silk stretchers, heavy with bales and boxes, between them.

013-Unidentifed seized a moment when his guard's head was turned to try to untie his leash, but the burly soldier who was holding the other end noticed and gave a terrible flick of the rope, which sent the young bird tumbling. "Don't you dare try anything like that once we arrive there!" The guard rushed the white bird along so quickly that he had no chance to try an escape again.

013-Unidentified was nearly breathless when they did.

The winter palace of the archaeopteryxes was a miniature forest on bamboo stilts. It rose out of the middle of a slimy pond. The platform above the stilts had been covered with earth, and plants that thrived in mild winters were planted in it. They grew in a thick screen that hid the actual halls and buildings from view. As Kawaka and his train approached the palace, all 013-Unidentified could see was an arched opening between two trees, leading to a long, shaded green tunnel.

"Sir Kawaka, reporting for the annual tribute. I request an audience with the Ancient Wing." Kawaka nodded at the gate guard. He felt the tension draining out of him now that he was safely at the winter palace. It was always dangerous carrying so many valuables across the Marshes. His train had been attacked this time by a ragtag band of herons, egrets, and kingfishers, although they'd beaten them off with little trouble.

The sentry at the gate looked over Kawaka and his officers and stepped back to let them pass.

Carrying the wooden box on his back, Kawaka, followed by his soldiers, passed through the green tunnel and into a bright hall filled with winter jasmine. He looked over his shoulder and gave 013-Unidentified's captor a quick frown, and the bird dragged the prisoner faster. Behind them came the string of gift-laden soldiers.

When they were in place, they all crouched and waited, 013-Unidentified forced down by two other birds. Scholars of the court stood on the left, knights on the right.

Solemn expressions were pasted onto faces as a low drumroll issued from the royal orchestra. "His Majesty, Emperor Hungrias!" hailed a small archaeopteryx, followed by the tooting of a bugle.

A large archaeopteryx in silk ruffles and a velvet suit sewn with glittering jewels swept a curtain dramatically aside and landed on a high whalebone perch in front of Kawaka. A golden ring that dangled from a hole drilled through his beak glinted in the light. "So!" the Ancient Wing said throatily, his eyes sweeping across the tribute that Sir Kawaka had brought. "So!"

"I have things of great value this year." Kawaka bowed down at the Ancient Wing's feet, smiling. "Your Majesty, I have fans of egret feathers for you, and I have this slave, this unidentified bird, of no known species." His claws rested on the wooden box, but he didn't yet speak of the yellow gem, hoping to save the best for last.

013-Unidentified was prodded forward, and a chorus of oohs and aahs came from the scholars. "Really?" Hungrias studied the scrawny white bird doubtfully. "He is the only one of his kind?"

The chief scholar of the court fluttered forward, armed with rulers and little hammers, and did a lengthy examination. He flipped through a heavy tome labeled *The Complete and Thorough Record of the Class Aves.* At length, he declared, "Yes, Your Majesty! This bird is not listed in the book! He resembles a dove, but has certain traits of seabirds. His feet are rather too muscled for a passerine, yet his head and neck clearly mark him as a woodbird . . ."

The Ancient Wing's tiny eyes shut in bliss. "My, my, this is even better than the two-headed rooster that I got last year! Very tasty he was, too!"

013-Unidentified yelled in protest. He tried to leap toward the emperor. "You shan't!" It was all he could think of to cry. His separation from his mother, Irene, his seasons of washing dirty dishes in the Marshes Battalion . . . had he suffered all *that* just so that this fat bird would have a content stomach? How many other birds had encountered the same fate?

Immediately two archaeopteryxes pushed him roughly to the ground. The Ancient Wing puffed up in anger. But then, a noise broke through the hallway.

Emperor Hungrias straightened as a spindly messenger burst from the hall. The bird's long tail dragged behind him and the wet feathers on it were torn and broken. "Message, Your Majesty, from Sir Rattle-bones," he gasped. Hungrias looked keenly interested, forgetting about the outburst of 013-Unidentified. Kawaka jumped.

"Go on," Hungrias ordered eagerly.

"He is on his way back from inspecting the lands across the Augoric Ocean. He sent me ahead. I am to inform you that Sir Rattle-bones has succeeded in obtaining one of the Leasorn gemstones. It is red!"

"A Leasorn gemstone!" Hungrias nearly toppled off of his whalebone perch. Inside the ruff around his neck, the feathers of his head were standing on end with excitement. "From the lowly birds' stories," he mumbled to himself excitedly, "they say there are seven of them. Is he sure?" he demanded of the messenger. "It's definitely a Leasorn?"

"Yes, Your Majesty."

Hungrias had never recovered from the disappearance of his son two years before. He grieved and ordered a fitting punishment for Sir Maldeor, but his heart was not satisfied. He brooded on the gemstones and the lowly birds' legends until an idea formed in his mind—if only he could find all the rest of the jewels, he felt, he would recover the young prince, too. He ordered his remaining knights to locate the gems and they hastened to obey. Now finally a stone was on its way to him! Hungrias grunted with pleasure. "Yes, yes, my little son will be back soon!" He turned back to the messenger, already forgetting that Kawaka was still present at his court. "When is Rattle-bones coming? Is there an estimated time?"

"He shall arrive at Castlewood four weeks from now at the earliest, or two months at the latest."

"Indeed! I must see to it that we depart my Winter Palace early this year, perhaps tonight." The Ancient Wing waved a wing to dismiss the messenger.

"Your Majesty!" Kawaka said, agitated. "I must mention the most important of my gifts to you! Look at this."

He opened the wooden chest that he had been holding. His hopes for making the last piece of tribute the best that the emperor owned had been dashed by the news from his brother, and it was all he could do to stop his teeth from gnashing.

"Oh!" all the scholars cried. The chief strode forward. "Is this what I think it is?"

Heads tipped forward at the glowing yellow stone nestled in the box. 013-Unidentified craned his neck to see as well.

"Your Majesty, the former knight Maldeor went miles out of the Plains territory to find a Leasorn gem that is orange, and now my dear brother Sir Rattle-bones has crossed an entire ocean to find the Leasorn gemstone that is red. But I"—Kawaka allowed himself a humble bow—"a mere regional knight, have searched in Your Majesty's own blessed territory and have found this beautiful yellow Leasorn."

As proof, Kawaka flipped the gemstone over gingerly, and a facet with carvings was revealed. The chief scholar placed a small piece of fine birch bark over the stone, took out a tiny stick of charcoal, and traced the strange script on it. 013-Unidentified could see the lines clearly as the scholar held the bark up to the light, but the odd marks meant nothing to him.

"Indeed, indeed, Your Majesty," said the chief scholar. "I do not recognize this script at all. Very strange, very strange indeed. I must study this further."

"*Two* Leasorn gems!" Hungrias fanned his wings happily. "What a year for tribute this has been! We must celebrate. Tell the cooks to prepare a special meal. Oh, yes"—he pointed a wing at 013-Unidentified—"we shall see what this one tastes like tonight! Be sure he is still alive when he is placed on the spit. It improves the flavor so much."

Dozens of pairs of hungry eyes fastened upon him

as 013-Unidentified was dragged off to the kitchen, where he was lashed to a metal pole over a fire. Slaves, turning their faces aside, slowly rotated the spit as flames crackled eagerly.

013-Unidentified fainted from the heat.

A righteous heart can beam a light in the darkest place.
—FROM THE OLD SCRIPTURE

3
CHOICE

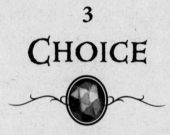

Gradually 013-Unidentified became aware that a raven was clacking his beak loudly. "Come," the raven rasped, beckoning. "Come, you don't want to be late."

"No!" 013-Unidentified whispered. For some reason, he didn't want to go anywhere with this stranger.

"Come," the bird insisted. "I've been ordered to bring you, and bring you I must. But if you ask, I must bring you back again. Those are the laws I obey."

Out sprang a claw that clasped around the white bird's neck. He gasped. His conscious soul was being lifted out of his body! The raven flew out of the kitchen. Nobird seemed to notice. 013-Unidentified turned back to look, and saw his body still on the fire.

"Where are we going?" he asked the raven, choking.

"To Yin Soul."

They flew over an endless stretch of gray, an angry ocean beneath them. It seemed only minutes before the raven dropped 013-Unidentified. He landed before he could open his wings.

He was in a small red room, the walls lined with looming bookshelves. On the far side was the red frame of a fireplace, surrounded with red incense and sputtering red candles. The sharp cinnamon perfume they gave off stung his eyes.

"Hello, dear 013-Unidentified." The youngster jumped at the sudden words; they were whispery and thin. A scaly creature in a broad red manteau nodded slightly as he scuttled from behind a pile of books. He looked a lot like an archaeopteryx, except he was larger and had four wings. "I am Yin Soul. Come here, young one, and perch beside me."

013-Unidentified obeyed in a dreamlike trance. The

carpet underfoot, woven with a design like red and yellow flames, felt so plush.

"I do feel very sorry for you." The creature's eyes softened with what looked like a fatherly fondness. "You were going to die. They wanted to cook and eat you; how cruel! But now you're here. You want to live, surely? *Everybird* wants to live!" Yin studied 013-Unidentified. He began again, quietly. "I like your spirit. Facing the reality bravely. But don't you want to fight your enemies? Don't you want to steer the flight of your life? I can save you from that fire. You'd be free."

013-Unidentified gaped. "Free! I—"

Yin Soul's eyes bore into 013-Unidentified's. "But being free is not enough. You know that your enemies deserve to be punished. They deserve to be punished for causing you pain, for every injustice, for every feather they tore loose. Some even deserve death! I know a way for that. Hero's Day is the day of the fifth full moon in a year and a half. You know the legends about a magical sword that can be found at Kauria, the Island of Paradise. If you find the sword on that particular day, you will have power over all your enemies. Then you can do what your heart tells you to do! All you must do is agree to swallow my essence."

After a silence, Yin glanced into the distance and sighed. "I am like you. I know how it feels. Truly." He smiled sadly at 013-Unidentified.

"Why do you want me to swallow your essence?" the white bird asked at last.

Yin Soul closed his eyes. "Then I would be able to

guide you from inside your body."

013-Unidentified peered at Yin Soul, confused. Suppose, just suppose it was real. Then his troubles would probably end here and now, but . . . was his conscience telling him no? Was it the same thing that had made him say his long-ago name, Wind-voice, instead of 013-Unidentified when he spoke to the woodpecker captive, Ewingerale?

You are Wind-voice, not 013-Unidentified, a voice deep inside him said. *Think like Wind-voice.*

For a split second, everything in the room changed. Red blurred to gray. The flames went out; the candles were pools of wax. The cinnamon scents of incense soured into those of spoiled fish.

The old, kind bird was transformed. The eyelids were gone, and Wind-voice could see his eyeballs, dark yellow as rotten plums. The gentle chuckles of Yin Soul changed to a dreadful sound, as if somebird was vomiting. This was what Yin Soul was truly like. The feathers on Wind-voice's nape rose and he gulped. He was chilled with fear. It was suddenly very cold.

The next second everything returned to the way it had been.

"013-Unidentified, will you agree?"

Wind-voice didn't dare to look into Yin Soul's face,

but he knew what he wanted to say. "No. Take me back! I want to go back." He rose and looked around. He saw the raven who had brought him here lurking behind a bookcase and stepped toward him. "Take me back to the archaeopteryxes."

"You cannot," Yin Soul taunted. With a whirl of his wings, the shadows of ghostly birds, screeching unearthly sounds, appeared out of nowhere and moved swiftly toward Wind-voice. "You cannot. It is against your instincts to go willingly to your death. Come to me!"

But Wind-voice knew—he had seen, in that brief moment of true sight—that Yin Soul's apparent kindness could not be trusted. Whatever he offered, whatever he planned, Wind-voice knew he wanted no part of it— even if the other choice was death.

Wind-voice faced the raven. "No! I want to go back! You said you must take me back!"

"I don't think so. Stay." Yin Soul rose as well and reached out a rootlike, quivering claw.

Wind-voice flung a red blanket at Yin Soul. Then he grabbed hold of the raven's feet and shouted, "Fly!" The raven cawed in surprise. The mangy bird dragged Wind-voice into the air as Yin Soul yelled below them, "Soon you'll wish you had listened to me!" The ghost birds wailed along with their master. Wind-voice didn't see Yin Soul shaking his balled claws, didn't hear him whisper, "At least there is the other one."

Wind-voice closed his eyes tightly and could hear only the beat of the raven's wings, which soon turned into the crackling of wood.

To his horror, he could smell salt and pepper on his body. Had it all been a dream? Coughing, he opened his eyes. His smothered skin was flushed to a reddish pink, and his lungs felt as if they had collapsed. He was still over the fire. Tears burst into his eyes as sparks leaped up and scorched him. But the tears quickly evaporated in the heat.

Wind-voice realized that there wasn't much smoke around him. But the smoke had to go out somewhere. Craning his neck, he squinted at the ceiling above. Cold air blew through a jagged hole. He looked around. No archaeopteryxes cared to be near the heat of the fire. The fire tenders were all away on errands for the cook at the moment. He peered down into the flames. There was only one way, and that was the fool's way. He opened his beak, sucked in a deep breath, and blew with all his might at the fire. Shutting his eyes tightly, he waited for the flames to flare back at him. He felt his ropes starting to char. But his feathers were burning as well.

One rope fell. He fluttered the freed wing awkwardly and leaned forward to peck at the ropes around his other wing. The ropes dropped into the flames and withered to ashes.

Summoning his ebbing strength, Wind-voice beat his wings and flitted toward the hole in the ceiling.

It was a tight fit, but he struggled madly. There was a rip. He was in the air, in the night air! The bitter wind welcomed him.

"It escaped!" cried an archaeopteryx below.

Wind-voice's body was blazing as he flew. The long sweeps of the flailing wings were sweeps of flame. He looked like a firebird.

The archaeopteryxes shot a volley of arrows at him, but they fell short.

He knew he could not last long in the air. His past was burning away. He could be what he wanted to be.

013-Unidentified is truly dead, he thought as his scorched body faltered and plummeted down. *Wind-voice is reborn.*

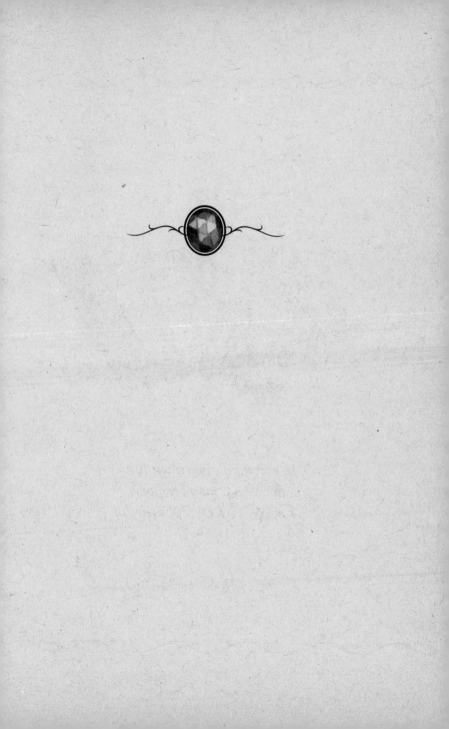

*In everybird's innermost heart
there lies a moral compass.*
—FROM THE OLD SCRIPTURE

4
BEGINNING

"Fly in low to the west, Wind-voice! Hide!" Irene, his mother, shouted. Frightened, he obeyed. His mother started flying in the other direction, jumping now and then, pausing a few times to let the archaeopteryxes catch up. She let one of her wings trail behind, feigning injury in a desperate attempt to draw away the enemy.

He stumbled in terror and looked back. Irene disappeared

from sight around a sand dune. The archaeopteryxes followed. It was the last time Wind-voice saw his mother.

Memory scorched Wind-voice along with the flames. He closed his eyes, trying not to scream, as the ground rushed up at him. His wings were useless. He twisted to land on his feet, and his right foot jammed full-force onto a rock. The rest of him crashed down onto it.

Though most of the flames had been beaten out by his crash, a few feathers were still smouldering. Then, to his surprise, a thin, high voice whispered in his ear. "Wind-voice! Thank the Great Spirit, you're alive!"

It was Winger. The woodpecker scooped up some cool, wet mud and put out the flames quickly, then smeared some more to blot out all of Wind-voice's white feathers so he would not be easily spotted. "Try to get up," Winger urged. "Quick, quick."

"Where can we go?" Wind-voice asked, staggering to his feet.

"I know where. Just come with me."

Wind-voice knew he could not fly. But he limped as fast as he could, trying not to put much weight on his injured claws, the woodpecker supporting him.

Wind-voice's vision began to blur and waver. Suddenly he saw the rich purplish black of another bird, a myna, who appeared beside Winger and helped Wind-voice walk. Supported by the two birds, he stepped into the fringe of golden light from a campfire and saw a gray-and-blue bird practicing the graceful movements of swordplay, all alone. Wind-voice flinched at the sight of the red and orange flames.

Bright flashes of green-blue filled the air as little kingfishers darted toward them. The stout myna congratulated Wind-voice on his daring escape. Ewingerale said something to him excitedly in his shrill little voice, but he couldn't catch the words. So many smiling faces loomed up at him. Some started bandaging his burns and washing his injured foot with cool water.

Then Wind-voice turned and saw two dull yellow sticks in front of his eyes. Numbly he realized they weren't sticks at all but spindly legs. There was an ugly scar on the right foot. He looked up to see folded wings and a body and, higher still, a long neck curving over and a pair of yellow eyes looking at him. It was the bird who had been practicing with the sword. The heron's white face was almost comically wedgelike, but the two bold, black brushstrokes sweeping up above the eyes, however, were just menacing enough to stop any laughter. He said in a deep, vibrant tone, "Welcome, son. You are safe here. I am the heron Fisher. Welcome."

With those words, the haze in Wind-voice's mind cleared.

"We're free now, we're free!" the woodpecker shouted joyously. Wind-voice noticed the myna, standing still but with one claw running up and down a long wooden staff. He flew over to the myna and thanked him. The myna made a slight inclination with his head. "Don't mention it. You're a tough one. My name is Stormac." Wind-voice was surprised to see that, despite his warriorlike appearance, Stormac sported a funny necklace with a red wooden pendant.

Wind-voice felt warmth that he had not thought existed in this forlorn, marshy land. "What tribe is this?" he croaked.

"These times are hard on tribes," answered the old heron, gesturing far and wide with both wide wings. "Several tribes, survivors of attacks by the archaeopteryxes, live together here as a community. We have egrets, mynas, and herons as well as the Ekka tribe of kingfishers."

Then another heron drifted over to them and handed them each a small, flat rock with steaming food on top. Everybody grew quiet at the sight of the heron. She seemed to be focused elsewhere. "Here," she said. They stammered their thanks.

The heron seemed to hear something nobird else did and wandered into the shadows, murmuring, "Candles . . . he made the best candles, even ones shaped like heron chicks. It's a pity, but those chick candles have all burned out . . ."

"That's my wife, Aredrem," Fisher said sadly, and went over to comfort her. "I was a candlemaker before the turmoil started. We lost all our children to archaeopteryxes or to hunger. I lost a toe in battle, so I cannot make candles as I used to. Poor Aredrem was shaken. She's in a different world now. But Aredrem seems to have taken a liking to you two."

How lost her face looks! She lost her children. I lost my mother. This is what war does to birds, Wind-voice thought sadly. He looked down at his plate. The delicious smell almost unnerved him. For a bird who had lived on spoonfuls of watery bulrush-root soup, this was a feast for a king. There were worms with chokeberries. The worms were long and thick, roasted to perfection. Brown and crisp, the skin had rich fat sizzling between the cracks, and the juicy meat still had a tint of pink. The chokeberries, boiled into a rosy sauce, brought out that tender, earthy flavor so unique to worms.

Between beakfuls of food, he and Winger told the marshland birds what had happened. "I burned myself off the spit and flew out of the smoke hole, flaming. Then, fortunately, Winger saved me," Wind-voice finished. He did not mention the strange dream of Yin Soul.

"Brave thing you did. That's the true spirit!" a kingfisher said, cheering.

"Aye! What a tale," an egret agreed.

"I think . . ." Ewingerale murmured tentatively, "I think I would like to play a song to celebrate this. Would you happen to have some spare bowstrings?" To the surprise and admiration of them all, the woodpecker fed the string into the holes of his piece of curved wood with deft precision and, in no time at all, held a harp.

Strumming it, the woodpecker sang,

Fate is an underground river,
We can't possibly know what direction it flows
Till we are carried along its twists and turns.
But the waters are quite smooth now,

Flowing quick and fast.
We are happy and thankful that
We're free—long may it last!
Let us hope that fate may bring
Wonderful things next spring.

His song flowed over the pools, which were pale green with a fine skin of duckweed. From them rose the crooked limbs of dead, bare trees. They were hung with curtains of Spanish moss, and their branches, sharp white wood, framed the sky like teeth. A few cold flakes of snow fell. It had been over twenty seasons since it last snowed here. It was both bizarre and beautiful, as if little stars in the vast, dark sky had decided to fall down.

"It's a pity, but those candles have all burned out . . ." Aredrem's voice floated in the darkness.

As the song faded, Fisher came over to Wind-voice. "Why don't you rest?" the heron asked.

"I'm afraid to," Wind-voice admitted. He turned to Fisher. "Suppose something eats you from your inside, trying to control you. Suppose it lures you to do something, and you know it is not at all good, but you also know that if you listen too long, you will believe. It's more dangerous than anything outside you. Perhaps the way to defeat it is never to give it a chance to speak to you." *Like Yin Soul, who promised me life in the face of death,* he thought. *Like fear, like despair, like greed, like anger.*

Fisher stared at the young bird. "After all you've been through, after living and struggling on when some would have just given up and died, nobird would dare try to force you to do something you didn't choose. I think that your experiences and choices have tempered you so that you can be the master of yourself." *Because your heart and soul have awakened,* Fisher thought.

He watched as a strange calmness came over Windvoice. Then the young bird spoke seriously. "Fisher?"

"Yes?"

"I saw you . . . practicing with the sword. There's Stormac with his staff. I think we all need to learn how to protect ourselves in the days to come. My foot . . . will I ever . . . ?" His voice trailed off. His right foot hung by his belly, the scales scratched and mangled. It was tinted purple with bruises and darkened blood within.

"Yes, yes, you will," the heron replied firmly.

For the first time that Fisher had seen, the white bird smiled, revealing his youthfulness. But it was not a brief smile of joy or hope. It said: *Fate lays a difficult path ahead for me. What I have done and what I am will shape my future.*

Smile on, little one. Always smile, Fisher thought.

Then the young bird fluffed up his feathers, crouched on his good foot, tucked his head beneath his wing, and slept.

Fisher slowly crept into the cedars, toward a hut made from planks of deadwood propped together. In it were the weapons of all the marshland birds. A crane sentry was stationed nearby. The crane stood with a rock held in his claws so that if he fell asleep while on duty, the rock would drop and he would be awakened. "Hello, Fisher," the crane said, understanding. He allowed the heron inside.

Fisher went to the back of the hut and bent down. Soon he straightened up again, holding a small sword of simple but graceful design. It was a blade that Fisher himself had wielded when he was young. Something light, quick, and true.

Then he crept back, the coals in the fire dimming, holding that small weapon. Gently he opened Wind-voice's balled claws and placed the sword's hilt into the palm. The young bird did not stir, but the bruised claws closed tightly around the hilt. Fisher wrapped his own spindly claws around Wind-voice's, feeling the power and strength of a determined young soul.

"Yes, yes, you will," he whispered again.

Hundreds of miles northeast, where a blizzard was sweeping across ancient forests of spruce and fir, a beggarbird teetered on top of a hill, a dark flea-sized dot on the white mound.

"Abandoned! Days and days, with shame for a hat and hunger for a coat. Nobird takes pity on me here. With one wing, am I even a bird anymore?" he shouted at the sky, his remaining wing raised. He waited angrily, but the storm only howled on. The dried maple leaves he had strung together and worn as a shirt rustled; brown-and-khaki tatters of his uniform on his gaunt frame below thrashed about in the wind. "No answer! You are like the rest. Always ignorantly scornful! Hateful!" The beggar wheezed. Wiping the dribble off his teeth, he lurched down the hill. The frostbitten and rotting stump of his left wing was bleeding again. Maggots writhed inside it, burrowing for warmth. "You eat me, I eat you," Maldeor growled. He picked a slimy white one out with his beak and swallowed it. "So hungry . . ." He tripped and fell. He lay still. The dark frozen mass of blood on his shoulder shone like a garnet, eerily beautiful among his filthy rags.

Gradually, snowflakes started to cover the beggarbird Maldeor, former head knight under Emperor Hungrias, now an exiled criminal.

Strong of body, clever of mind, tactical, daring, but downtrodden enough to be vulnerable. Yin Soul had devoted every second to finding a bird matching this description. He needed a bird who would be clever enough to find the hero's sword but still weak enough to take Yin Soul's essence into himself. After his failure with Wind-voice, he still had Maldeor to fall back on, but he was afraid—afraid that Maldeor would recognize him as the one who had eaten the prince. "He won't," Yin Soul grumbled, and took care to rearrange his manteau before sending his raven messenger to fetch the archaeopteryx. *I have to be more careful this time and not reveal everything all at once,* Yin Soul thought.

Revenge. Power. Strength. Yin Soul promised Maldeor all of these.

"Look at yourself. A knight, reduced to a crippled criminal. Your eyes spew flame while they glaze, even now, in death."

"Don't taunt me."

"Feisty, aren't you? Here you have two paths ahead. One you know: death. But I can still provide another. Once I was like you. I was robbed of my potential and power by Yama and the Great Spirit and forever bound in this accursed place between the living world and the dead. But I can help you find the power I never had."

Maldeor did not look up at all. After his wing had been chopped off, his face had developed a permanent grimace. "I'm waiting to die. Let me die. I'm not going to live in the agony and shame of a one-winged bird."

"You would die and let your enemy, Hungrias, triumph? I can give you a wing. It's not a normal wing, but it shall fit you even better than the one you lost." In the shadows, Yin Soul raised his wing and hacked swiftly down. His turned face shielded his expression of pain as one hind wing came off of his ghostly body. *It is worth it,* he thought, gritting his teeth. He hunched over and hopped forward into the light again. His manteau was long and wide enough to hide his missing wing.

"Here," he said, choking, and raised a bony wing almost like a bat's, with shimmering hairs growing out of pale scales that stretched over it. "Something neither sword nor arrow can destroy. It will let you fly once more. You can truly be a bird again."

Maldeor longed for it. To fly again, to have power over those who'd done this to him . . . but something was wrong with this offer. He knew it. He batted the wing off to one side.

Yin Soul paused. He stepped forward and slowly drew a claw out from his tattered sleeve. He tenderly laid it on Maldeor's blood-splattered head and turned it upward. As he gazed into Maldeor's glazed eyes, two shining tears rolled slowly down Yin Soul's thin cheeks. A flame hissed in the background.

"Look what they have done to you." His voice rippled. "Look what they have done to the world, these evil birds with nothing but their own power and pleasure in their hearts. Don't you want to stop them? Won't you let me help you?"

He looked as if he grieved for Maldeor's pain, for all the pain in the world. As if he knew what the archaeopteryx was suffering. As if he truly cared.

"Please." Maldeor believed that Yin Soul was sincere. His suspicions melted away and he broke down at last. "Please save me. Help me."

How was he to know that Yin Soul truly cared for nobird but himself?

"As I am tied here, I cannot interfere directly in the affairs of mortals," Yin Soul told Maldeor. "But I know much. The wing will help you fly again. See if you like it. But it is only a spirit wing, not made of mortal flesh. Every month, on the night of the new moon, you must return here, and I will give you a potion. You must drink it to give the wing strength. And, I will have something better for you later on. To shape the world into that of our vision, you will need the sword, the one the Great Spirit commanded Pepheroh to make. It's hidden on the island of Kauria. I can give you one clue: Hero's Day is on the day of the fifth full moon in a year and a half. However, there is a strange white bird called 013-Unidentified, who I feel poses a threat to your goals. Find and kill him. Then search for the gemstones, Leasorn gems, as some call them. They will give you the rest of the clues you need." Yin Soul raised two wings upward. "That sword is waiting for a hero to wield it. It has the power to do anything . . . everything."

*If you kill a thousand birds, you win a forest,
yet if you kill an emperor, you own an empire.*
—FROM THE *BOOK OF HERESY*

5
SOON, SOON

When Maldeor awoke, he jumped from the snow and tried to beat the air. The wing Yin Soul had given him worked. A malicious, gleeful cry tore from his throat.

Having traveled along in Hungrias's court during the winters when he had been a knight, he knew Hungrias was south in the Marshes Battalion. He took off in that direction, feeling his excitement rise with the temperature.

Hours later, he was in a discussion with Kawaka.

"I can't believe it! You are still alive, and flying!" Kawaka said gladly. Hungrias had threatened to demote him because the unidentified slave had escaped. Now here was Maldeor, the great knight who had also been wronged by the emperor.

"Follow me and overthrow Hungrias, Kawaka. When I am emperor I shall make you head knight."

"My soldiers and I shall serve you with all our hearts," Kawaka vowed. "I remember the day when Hungrias ordered us to hack off your wing. We all knew that the loss of the prince wasn't your fault. Soon, he will pay for the injustice."

For Wind-voice, the days in the marshland birds' camp were the best he'd ever known. His wounds healed, and Fisher taught him how to wield the sword that had once belonged to the heron. Wind-voice learned quickly and found courage in the quick slashing movements, in the brightness of the steel as it sliced through the air.

It was not only the training that gave him happiness but also his newfound friendships. When he was not playing his harp, Winger flitted around the field where Wind-voice practiced with Fisher, calling out encouragement. Stormac often came and practiced handling his

staff alongside his friends.

But the time couldn't last, and Wind-voice knew it. "I can't stay here. What if the archaeopteryxes started looking for me? I don't want to draw trouble onto your heads, especially after all your kindness to me."

Winger had been writing in a diary, and now he looked up. "Wherever you go, I will go."

"I will come, too," Stormac said.

"You are welcome to stay with us," Fisher told them. But when they insisted on leaving, Fisher sketched a map in the mud at his feet with one of his long toes. "The frontier territories beyond are safer. The archaeopteryxes are less numerous there. Near the Amali River you might find Fleydur, the eagle. There are other rebel groups across the river. He can take you to one or the other, if you wish to continue the fight against the archaeopteryx empire. But you don't have to do so. You can strike out on your own if you choose. Find a peaceful place, if you can, where you can live out your lives. Nobird would blame you. This fight is a hard one, and we may never win it by ourselves."

Stormac scowled. Winger turned away, a look of longing on his face. But Wind-voice faced Fisher in surprise.

"Do you truly think that?" he asked. "That we cannot win?"

Fisher sighed. His long beak drooped. "I would not say this to many. There are great deeds to be done, young ones, but quite frankly, we alone cannot do them. We have no power or strength, though we take action in our dreams and hearts. The path ahead is too treacherous." He stared into the sky. "But there is a hero who will succeed. He is coming . . . he is coming, and when he comes, he will release us from the claw of tyranny."

"Who is he?" Wind-voice's words were shaky.

"I don't know his name, and his face is unclear. But he

is coming, I know. When he comes, he will rescue the thousands of birds who are forced to live in hiding in barren lands. He will find good land for those birds to plant and harvest, and fill shriveled bellies. All birds will live side by side in peace."

Ewingerale looked up and listened as well, his eyes hungering.

"If we had our gemstone, I would know more." Fisher sighed. "That was a great loss. They say that gems like our Leasorn are supposed to hold clues to where a sword can be found, a sword that the hero will need."

"A sword? How can a weapon bring about peace?" asked Winger.

"It seems like a paradox," agreed the heron. "But it is not a war sword. Its hidden power will shake the evil. In the claws of the hero, it will bring happiness to us."

Wind-voice looked up wistfully and asked, "When is this hero coming?"

The silence was cruel. "Soon, Wind-voice," the heron said. "Soon."

Maldeor perched in the midst of Kawaka' s soldiers, gazing quietly at the gate of the archaeopteryx emperor's winter castle. A hood was pulled low over his eyes and a cloak hid everything but his scrawny claws. Snow fell, but he was still.

Kawaka called out. Inside the gatehouse, an archer guard opened a small peephole. "What do you want in the middle of the night?" he demanded. "If you have a message to leave, be quick."

"I have a special message," Kawaka said. "It is only for the Ancient Wing's ears." The guard surveyed the group. He was about to let them in when he saw Maldeor. *Who is he?* he wondered. Before he could ask, Maldeor raised his left wing slightly. The cloak he was wearing rippled away and left the wing bare.

The guard swallowed. By the light of the moon, he saw moist gray skin. Beneath it, masses of blood vessels throbbed in and out of sight, as if challenging him. Though the rest of the creature's body was still, the shiny black claws on the foot coming off the arc of his wing twitched.

Whoever he is, he's with Kawaka, so it must be safe to let him in, thought the guard with a shiver. After a series of clicks, slowly the door opened a crack.

Maldeor walked briskly in with Kawaka by his side and headed down the long green tunnel, past the lighted torches and trophies, past the soldiers on night duty and the servant birds. The scrawny head scholar he had bribed gave him a slight nod. Nobird attempted to stop him or question him. Maldeor turned before he came to the audience hall hung with jasmine, where Hungrias had received his tribute not long before. Down the left hall, up three branches, left again in the corridor, then right. There was no doubt or hesitation as he came to the final grand door, opened it, and slipped in.

The emperor of Archaeopteryxes stood alone by his window, yawning, moonlight catching on the ring that hung from his beak. His body was swathed in a robe of red velvet, silk, and gold trim, and he still held a slice of crab pinched between two talons.

"I'm back, Ancient Wing," Maldeor said.

The olive green feathers on the emperor's neck stood on end. Beak ring jangling, he spun around and met a sight that made the crab tumble from his claw.

"You—" Emperor Hungrias gasped, eyes bulging.

"Yes, me."

"You're still alive . . ." the emperor stammered. "Your w-w-wi—"

Maldeor unclasped his damp cloak, the faintest of smiles flickering across his face. The cloth, maroon with a silver lining, fell in a glossy heap at his feet. He shook off the remaining snow. Maldeor raised his left wing. The Ancient Wing stared.

"By my teeth, how could—" Again the emperor broke

off his sentence, and again Maldeor smiled.

"Why are you here?" gasped Hungrias at last, the green feathers on his fat cheeks trembling.

"Don't we both know?" his gray companion sneered. His sharp white teeth glittered like crystals.

The emperor clutched the windowsill. It seemed best to vault out and flap away into the snowy darkness, but—no. "You murderer. And liar!" He propelled his fat body forward. "You killed my son. You lost the gemstone. You lied to me. Do you think that I am so foolish as to believe your crazy story of some four-winged dinosaur? Ha! Disappearing in flames . . . How dare you come back here!"

"I did not lie! I told the truth. You destroyed me," Maldeor said, and for a moment his stiff calm evaporated. "I did nothing but serve you. All the knights of the court pleaded for me when I came back. You know they would have fought against you if you beheaded me, so you cut off my wing instead. You expected me to die. I didn't. It was hate and vengefulness that somehow dragged me up from death. Do you know how I suffered, my stump constantly bleeding? I had been your best and most loyal knight. Who knows what other cruelties you have committed? Or what you will inflict on others in the future? *I* shall show you what an emperor should be."

"Guards!" the emperor cried furiously. "Take him away!"

Maldeor laughed. "Didn't your servants tell you that they had a message from Sir Kawaka? He has agreed to serve me now. His birds have overpowered your guards. Your court wishes for a new emperor to follow."

There came a tapping on the door. Maldeor quickly

put on his heavy cloak again before opening it. Instead of the emperor's guards, Kawaka walked in. Beside him was the chief scholar of the court. Other knights and scholars flanked them. Armed birds from Kawaka's battalion pressed in close behind.

With an angry stare, Hungrias tore out his beak ring and tossed it at Maldeor's claws. "Take it! Take it!"

Calmly Maldeor bent and scooped it up with one claw. He held it up. It was pure gold, finely crafted, with a single dark onyx sphere caught in a web of gold twine. Along one edge were inscribed the words RULER OF THE TOOTH-BEAKED.

"Thank you, Ancient Wing," said Maldeor, pocketing it. "I accept this responsibility. I will command your battalions. I will bring peace and order to the world. Everything will be under my control. There will be no more evil. There will be an end to birds like you."

"I can't believe . . . you rascal, you criminal . . ." Hungrias huffed.

Maldeor ignored him.

Maldeor smiled serenely at the knights and scholars. He raised a claw and jingled the beak ring once.

"Ancient Wing," shouted the scholars, the knights, and the soldiers. Each thumped his left foot on his chest feathers in the archaeopteryx gesture of loyalty. That was all that was needed for a new emperor to rise.

The soldiers behind them echoed the gesture. "Ancient Wi—"

With a crash, Hungrias leaped forward with spider-like venom, a hidden sword drawn out and pressed against Kawaka's throat. "Traitor . . ."

Hungrias never finished his sentence. There was a metallic blur behind him, and he toppled, his sequined doublet now shining dully.

"That old spider had tricks, always," Maldeor said, sheathing his own sword. He had used his specialty, the Deadly Fate move, which seldom failed. He ruffled his feathers, then continued. "Send out word to every battalion that they have a new emperor now," Maldeor ordered. "I have plans for them all. First, we will leave this place as soon as possible and return to Castlewood. This winter palace is for weaklings. Enduring the cold winter will strengthen us." He glanced scornfully at the body of Hungrias.

"Yes, Your Majesty." The head scholar walked up, holding a piece of paper in his claws. "But before we go, Your Majesty, do you wish us to circulate the new list of wanted birds that Hungrias issued?"

Maldeor was about to snap "No!" but changed his mind. "Read off the names." He listened intently.

Suddenly the words "013-Unidentified" made him jump. *Yin Soul, my mentor, spoke of this bird!* he thought. "Yes, 013-Unidentified, I want him!" Maldeor barked. "Double the reward of acorns and pine seeds. Make sure you put a sketch of his face on the posters. What crime did he commit?"

"He yelled openly at Hungrias and escaped against Hungrias's wishes."

Maldeor nodded and stored this information in his head. *One thing at a time,* he thought. *Next, Kauria.* He spun around, turning to the chief of the scholars. "All right then, what do you know about Kauria?"

The old archaeopteryx blinked in surprise. "Kauria? It is a legend, my lord, a mythical island where snow never falls and the flowers never fade, ruled by a phoenix, Pepheroh. But it is a just a story. Nobird with any learning thinks it truly exists." He faltered a little under Maldeor's stern glare.

"It exists," Maldeor said fiercely. "And I will find the way there. Search your books and scrolls. Tell me anything you find. All of you!" His gaze traveled across the group of birds.

"Your Majesty, here is a yellow Leasorn gem, which Kawaka had brought." The head scholar raised the gemstone that had been stolen from the kingfishers.

The words are in Avish . . . I must learn the language in time and decode them, Maldeor thought. Feeling better, he thundered on. "Now then, anybird you meet, soldier or slave, who knows anything of Kauria—I want to speak to that bird. Let that order go out to every archaeopteryx in the land. Is that understood?"

"Aye, Ancient Wing." They all bowed.

The world is in my claws, Maldeor thought as he rolled the beak ring slowly in his talons, back and forth, back and forth.

Chaos can cast a shadow on one's conscience.
—from the OLD SCRIPTURE

6

BEWILDERED

Wind-voice, Stormac, and Ewingerale flew along the edge of a small woodland. Suddenly Wind-voice, in the lead, ducked into the shadows of a thicket. The other two followed. Silently Wind-voice gestured with his beak toward an archaeopteryx ahead in a clearing, nailing a poster to a tree with a thorn.

After the toothed bird had gone, Ewingerale went up

and read the words on the paper out loud.

"'It is proclaimed that the head of 013-Unidentified, a bird white of feather with red bill and feet, is wanted by the Marshes Battalion as well as the new Ancient Wing . . .' See?" whispered Ewingerale. "Your head is worth twenty bushels of acorns and pine seeds, plus a bag of treasure!" He looked up in shock.

"A lot, when you think about it, in early spring," Stormac muttered.

"That's not all." Ewingerale read on. "'Along with the aforesaid Unidentified bird, one woodpecker, number 216, and one myna, number 987, are wanted and are highly suspected to be accomplices . . .'"

"We'll have to be more careful than ever," Wind-voice said. "Everybird will be looking for us now."

Wind-voice was right. The swordcraft he had learned from Fisher was put to the test quite soon. As they were flying near the shores of a lake, five dark shapes suddenly melted from the trees. The commander, who was wielding a halberd, was in the lead. Two birds, armed with matching falchions, flanked him to the rear so the three formed a V. Between those two flew an archaeopteryx with a spear, and another, spinning a slingshot, brought up the rear.

In combat, the stocky leader would hack with his halberd at whatever was in front of him. At his signal, the two birds with falchions would rush forward and block victims from escaping to the left or right. The spear bird would dive down underneath to the other side to fight from the back while the archaeopteryx with the slingshot would fly overhead to shoot down hard round stones. It was grimly effective, and it was exactly what they did as they discovered the wanted birds: 013-Unidentifed, 216-Woodpecker, and 987-Myna.

The falchion-wielding bird on the left struck Wind-voice as familiar. He whirled to face him, bringing his sword to a guard position. The soldier attacked. Wind-voice dodged, but his foot was nicked.

He recognized the face of Dubto. "013-Unidentified!" the archaeopteryx called.

"You were kind to me once!" Wind-voice cried. "Why do you want to kill me now?"

"It's the command of the new Ancient Wing."

"But . . . why listen to him? Why not listen to your heart?"

"He has the beak ring. It is the age-old custom." Dubto's face shone with fierce loyalty. "Archaeopteryxes must follow whoever wears it."

"This is . . ." Wind-voice looked bewildered. "What about yourself? What would you choose for yourself?"

"I—" Dubto whispered, but he did not finish, for in that instant Stormac swept up and thumped his staff on the archaeopteryx's shoulders. Dubto plummeted away into the water below. Wind-voice looked around. The other soldiers had fallen as well and were struggling to rise again through the spray of water. Archaeopteryxes were powerful fighters but clumsy flyers.

"Looks like you have trouble dealing with that one. Just lending a wing," Stormac said cheerfully above the noise of the splashing water.

Wind-voice was dumbstruck. "You almost killed him!"

Stormac hovered, bewildered. "Wind-voice! They were sent to kill you! The archaeopteryxes nearly roasted you! Have you forgotten?"

"Hurry!" shouted Winger. "We must fly!"

Confused, Wind-voice matched wing beats with his companions till the archaeopteryxes could no longer be seen through the screen of lakeside trees. Was he fighting for revenge now? A picture formed behind his eyes: He, as an old warrior perched on a hill, saying, "Yes! I made him pay for that," and checking off a grudge out of a list so long that it tumbled down the mountain slope. *Is this what my life would be?* he thought, troubled.

Later that night, by their tiny campfire, Ewingerale came up to Wind-voice. Without a word, he carefully used a few strips torn from his vest to bind up the wound on Wind-voice's foot. "Nothing is clear in life," he whispered. Then, sitting back, he tuned his harp and started playing and singing a little song:

Why do we fight?
We often don't know.
Isn't the reason we fight murky like stew?
Thick like split-pea porridge.
We often don't know what's false and what's true,
Just face it with some courage.

Wind-voice listened mournfully. He tried to smile back at Winger. The song helped a little, but confusion still swirled in his head. Had Stormac's warrior logic been correct? Could it be truly right to kill a bird who had once been kind to him, even if that bird had been sent to kill him now? Or was there some other way?

As they traveled on, they passed fresh ruins of homes. Once they saw birds gathered together in an eerie cemetery, staring at the sky. "We'll join the dead soon, we'll join the dead soon," a wren bawled. Vultures spanned overhead. When Stormac called to the mourners, asking what had happened, they only said, "Maldeor's back."

"Who is Maldeor?" Stormac demanded.

No answer.

"A league away, there are more carcasses." They could faintly hear the croak of one vulture to another.

"I don't care!" the second vulture howled from the

ground beside a still body. He looked wildly about. "For a long time I was glad the archaeopteryxes had taken over. Rotting carcasses that were unburied and unclaimed were bountiful. But it's different when one of them is my own murdered sister."

Wind-voice and his friends helped the stricken vulture bury his sibling. Winger cried softly:

The howling wind carries away our elegies.
Behold: white bones piled up at the graveyard,
Unburied.
Dear ones killed,
Neither by gods of thunder nor plague
But by toothed birds.
Can wailing call them back?
Can mourning comfort their souls?
Only ghostly songs echo.

We can't let this happen—the world, turning into a graveyard! Wind-voice thought. "I must find the hero and help stop the archaeopteryxes," he said aloud.

The marshland grew drier, turning into a forest. Wind-voice's injured foot worsened. The wound had gotten infected, and the foot was beginning to swell. Stormac asked directions of a small, frightened hummingbird, who told them the way to a beech tree in a thicket where a healer, a shrike named Rhea, could be found.

Just outside her bush, Rhea, wearing a faded purple shawl, sat tending to the wounded birds. When Wind-voice showed Rhea his right foot, she applied a pungent paste to it and bandaged it. "Here, drink this and you will feel better." The delicate old shrike gave Wind-voice a cup of crabapple cider. "There is something I must attend to. Rest here as long as you wish."

She went deeper into her thorny bush.

Wind-voice wondered if it was his imagination, but he heard faint murmurings, as if from voices in the distance. Then a small finch, one wing wrapped in a clumsy bandage, came through the door and asked for the healer.

"She went through there," Wind-voice said, and hobbled over to call her. He found that the murmuring voices grew louder as he went farther into the bush. From the wide eyes of Stormac and Ewingerale, he knew they heard them too.

They ducked under a low branch of the bush and found themselves inside a tree. The bush concealed a secret entrance to the beech tree, which had a hollow trunk. Cracks in the bark above let in light. Many birds were crowded into the hole, some with battle scars, some wearing the robes of scribes. Young and old alike perched, listening. Not all were forest birds. A sandpiper twitched uncomfortably in a pile of wood chips. A bright lyrebird made a splash of color in the corner.

The three companions slid into the back row, concealing themselves behind a dry old branch with a pointed tip.

"...as I have said, a new threat seems to be gathering," a troubled chiffchaff was saying. "That knight, Maldeor, the one who lost the prince and was abandoned to die, is alive. And he's back. It's rumored that he dethroned Hungrias himself! He's searching, too, searching for something, and killing whatever gets in his way. You all know of his notorious Deadly Fate move."

"What should we do, then? How can we protect ourselves?" one of the younger birds said.

The dry old branch beside the three listeners suddenly became animated. The pointy tip opened and said, "Aye! Tell us!" The thing was not wood at all but a bird, a tawny frogmouth, so camouflaged that they had not recognized him.

A gruff voice rang out. It belonged to a proud old mockingbird. "I'll tell you what we must *not* do. A false notion spreads fast. Put a drop of ink into water and pretty soon everything's cloudy. Some have the false idea that we can ally ourselves with the archaeopteryxes. The Three Brethren have done it already. See where it has gotten them! The crows and ravens and mynas are no better than servants."

Wind-voice heard Stormac, beside him, draw in a sharp breath.

"If you befriend them, they'll turn on you or use you like a tool," the mockingbird went on. "We must stay apart from them. Don't be sympathizers or weaklings."

"You speak in generalizations," Rhea the healer argued. "'They,' 'we'? We are all birds, all of the class Aves. Can an entire race truly be evil?"

"Well, yes, I suppose you have some individuals who are different," the mockingbird conceded. "But just a few; and how important are those few? Most are our enemies and must be destroyed. Yes, there is another false notion that we must guard against: the idea that help will be arriving soon. There is no help but ourselves. Believe in such a thing and we'll be languishing, vulnerable. We must—"

Wind-voice crept out from behind the frogmouth. "But a hero is coming! We just have to prepare for him and help him."

"Hero?" the mockingbird sneered. "Who? Where is

this hero? Why hasn't he shown up before now?"

"I don't know," said Wind-voice. "But when he comes—"

"Where did you come from?" the mockingbird demanded. "Who let you in here?"

A young eagle stood up. "Sir . . . please. He's got a wound. Rhea was—"

The mockingbird stood, his wing tips flicking in anger, white patches flashing. "Were you hatched yesterday? This hollow, why, it belongs to us, the seasoned and aged. You can't even hold a sword properly. What made you think you have the right to speak here?"

"I will not have my patient mistreated," Rhea said, and stood up as well.

"He's the unidentified bird!" the frogmouth shouted. "Those three, they are the ones from the posters . . . the ones the archaeopteryxes want."

"See? See? Getting yourselves into trouble. Calling attention to yourselves, and then coming here to risk our lives as well!" the old mockingbird spluttered. "Nowadays youths think wars and battles are fun and games!"

As the meeting broke into an argument, Wind-voice stood still, shocked. Ewingerale was blinking rapidly, looking flustered. "Why don't these birds understand what we want to do," he whispered.

Wind-voice shrugged miserably. "I guess it's because I look so different. I belong to no species. We're younger than they are. We don't carry their bias."

Just then the young eagle sidled through the crowd and made his way to Wind-voice and his companions. "Come on now, my laddies, this is not a good time. Quickly!" The eagle brought them through Rhea's thicket and back to the outside world. "Don't mind the mockingbird. Can't blame him, poor bird, he lost his son and daughter to the archaeopteryxes. But you three had better get out of sight. Too many eyes and ears here."

Stormac remembered Fisher telling them of an eagle friend when they left. "Are you Fleydur?" he asked.

"Of course!" Fleydur smiled gaily. A broad, braided band of ribbons interwoven with all sorts of beads and small medallions crossed one shoulder. On it hung clusters of silver bells.

"Fisher told us about you. He said you'd help us cross the river," Wind-voice said.

"I know he did. I got a message three days ago. I suppose you've had to travel slowly and keep out of sight." The eagle checked the position of the sun. "Now, now . . . I imagine he meant for you to cross the Amali River into the Dryland. Archaeopteryxes are fewer there. Yes indeed, I will see you safe all the way. Now," he added, looking into a knapsack, "the checkpoint is several miles east of here. You three wear these." He produced several frills and bells to be hung over their shoulders.

Stormac saw a sack of tiny tinsel stars among the eagle's odds and ends. "Those shiny things!" the myna exclaimed. "What are they for?"

"To toss in my performances," Fleydur said cheerfully. Then his eye fell on Ewingerale's harp. "Just my luck! A harpist! A singer needs music. I'm not so good at instruments. I had a trumpet once, but it got broken in a scuffle. I haven't had the opportunity to make or get another one, but it will surely be good to have a harp along!"

"You sing?" Ewingerale seemed delighted. "That's wonderful. I can play ballads to go along. . . ."

Wind-voice felt his own tattered heart swell with joy and hope. Stormac grinned too. Later on he told Wind-voice, "He may pretend to be a simple bard, but I can tell he's got some training under his feathers. It will be great to have an extra fighter with us." He frowned. "But still, I've never seen an eagle this far from the safety of the mountains. And I don't know why he claims he's an orphan. I'm sure Fisher said something different. I don't suppose it matters, but it's odd, don't you think?"

Seven miles farther they arrived at the river. A thick stand of willow trees, cattail banks, and bulrushes was filled to the brim with archaeopteryxes. Many armed birds patrolled the riverside, for this place marked the end of the territory that was firmly under the archaeopteryxes' control. Most of the birds allowed past the river were those who had special permission from a highly ranked archaeopteryx. Merchant birds, once they paid a tax from their wares, came and went a little more easily; bards such as Fleydur could travel more or less freely.

Wind-voice nervously tapped his claw. He looked around and saw birds waiting for their chance to cross, sitting in groups. Some seemed to have been there a long time.

Fleydur had made them wait, hidden in the cattails, until the sun set and a crescent moon was rising, casting only a faint light. Now the four friends stood in a line of birds. Colorful berry stains had been smeared on their feathers. Wind-voice was no longer white, and Winger's bright red head had been blackened. Each of their shuffling steps jingled bells.

Wind-voice saw a small finch yanked out of the line by a beefy archaeopteryx. The finch didn't return.

Wind-voice and his companions stepped closer to the light cast by a ring of lanterns. Ten pairs of eyes stared at them. Ten toothed beaks glinted at them.

"We are birds of the music trade," said Fleydur. "I have the best voice in the Forests and the Marshes, and my good fellow tradesbirds here . . . well, let us show you!"

Waveringly they broke into song, looking at each other, soon smiling as they trilled. Fleydur did a spectacular sword-swallowing feat while Stormac tossed sparkling tinsel stars into the sky. Somehow the song made them feel a bit more courageous. Ewingerale plucked at his little harp. The eagle and the myna started whirling in a circle. Every few seconds, the two spinning, dancing figures blocked Wind-voice's view of the archaeopteryx soldiers standing and hovering there. He sang numbly, almost mechanically, as he saw silvery bells move up and down in front of him . . . then the staring pale eyes of the archaeopteryxes, then the bells again, then the eyes, until he thought they were one and the same . . .

It was really only a matter of a few minutes, although it seemed like a lifetime. They were ignored and roughly pushed outward to the tossing air currents above the river.

They still sang a little as they flew, partly for the archaeopteryxes' hearing, partly for themselves. Then their song faltered and died. Wind-voice's heart felt hollow. They'd crossed the river. He should feel triumphant; but what could they do now? Where would their path lead them?

Remorse for the past
enables us to do better in the future.
—FROM THE OLD SCRIPTURE

7
SECRETS REVEALED

Maldeor sat back in his newfound throne and gave a throaty chuckle. His army had captured a strange traveler. Soldiers had searched him and found a silver badge. It had a curved P surrounded by flowing tropical flowers. None of his officials thought it worth much attention, but the design of the badge had sparked an idea in Maldeor's head. Could P stand for Pepheroh, the ruler of Kauria?

There was a hubbub among the archaeopteryxes, and even the dignified officials stretched their necks to get a clearer view as the prisoner was brought before the throne. The bird had blue eyelids, a black nape and back, and a face and bib the color of a ripe banana. He was stocky and thickly muscled. The beak, or whatever it was, was shockingly ridiculous: Not only did it look heavy and was as long as the rest of the creature's body, but it also had a green base that merged into yellow with a magenta tip. "Is it painted?" somebird whispered.

"What is it?" Maldeor said.

"Your Majesty," declared a scholar as he took out a piece of rope and measured lengths, then looked through his copy of *The Complete and Thorough Record of the Class Aves*, "this is a toucan."

Maldeor held the silver badge in his claw. The toucan

immediately focused on it, his blue-rimmed eyes steady.

"Where are you from?" Maldeor asked softly.

"Nowhere," the toucan, who was Ozzan from Kauria, answered.

"Nonsense!" Maldeor leaned forward on his perch. "Where, exactly? An island, perhaps?"

After a pause for thought, the toucan nodded.

"Tell me its name."

There was silence.

"Speak up," Maldeor ordered. "There's plenty to talk about today. The island that you come from. The gemstones, the sword, and the legend."

"I will not," the toucan said after a long silence. His heavy accent grated the air.

Maldeor shook his head slowly as if confronted with a naughty hatchling. "I'm afraid," he said almost sadly, "that you will certainly reveal everything you know."

"So," said Fleydur once the traveling companions had found a safe perch for the night, "now that we are across the river, what are your plans? Where will you go?" His silver bells glowed in the moonlight as he settled in the lee of a cactus.

Stormac looked up from the beechnuts he had been

roasting. "Back to the herons, I suppose. They are my tribe now." He popped a kernel into his beak and swallowed dejectedly.

Winger was writing in his diary. He closed it carefully and put it into his large pocket, then looked sadly into the distance, strumming a few chords on his harp.

"I'm not sure. Where can we go? Wind-voice, what do you think? Should we try to find the rebels here on this side of the river? Maybe we can still join the fight and make some kind of difference."

Wind-voice was looking into the flames of their fire as if he could find an answer there. "I wish . . ."

"Wish what?" Stormac said. "Wishes find no beetles for breakfast."

"Don't say that." Winger leaned forward to look at Wind-voice. "What are you thinking?"

"I wish that we could do something to find the hero Fisher mentioned," Wind-voice said. "We need him so badly. How much longer can we wait?"

Winger shrugged. "But what can we do?"

The coals glowed peachy orange and fiery vermilion, but the flames flickered a bright, clear yellow hue. The color reminded Wind-voice of something. He had seen it in between the claws of the archaeopteryxes' emperor. Yes, a shining yellow stone, the amber gem of the king-fishers.

"The Leasorn gemstones," he said thoughtfully. "Fisher said that some birds believe they have clues. Clues about where the hero's sword might be hidden."

"Huh," Stormac snorted. "Made-up clues about a mythical sword. What help would that be to anybird?"

"Don't be so quick to dismiss the idea," Fleydur said, considering. "I've heard the same thing from bards of every land. Even my own tribe of eagles in the Skythunder Mountains has a gemstone, and it's true,

there were strange markings on it in some language—
Avish, I think."

"The kingfishers' amber stone has markings as well,"
Wind-voice recalled. "I saw one of the scholars of the
court copy them down." His claws twitched as he tried to
remember, and he scratched a few marks in the dirt. "It
was something . . . something like this . . ."

The others peered down at the lines he had drawn.

"The great clue looks like somebird scratching for
worms," Stormac said, amused.

"No, no, it doesn't!" Winger said, excited. "Look, look
here, Wind-voice. Could it have been like this?" He
rubbed out a few of Wind-voice's lines and drew them
again, slightly differently.

After looking at them for a long time, Wind-voice
nodded. "Yes. Yes, that's right. How did you know?"

Winger's voice shook. "My father was a scholar. He
was teaching me a written language like this before the
archaeopteryxes came and destroyed our tribe. This is
Avish, like Fleydur said, and it's the language from which
all bird languages are derived. It's used as a *lingua franca*
among learned birds. The written language is harder,
though. This says, 'The eye of the bird sees your wish.'"

Winger paused as memory flooded his brain. He
spoke rapidly. "I had just mastered Avish when the

archaeopteryxes attacked my tribe. They wanted to know about Avish. My father refused to tell them and fought to the death. They killed my mother and my sister. I wanted to die with them, but an archaeopteryx enslaved me for my harp music and forced me to live on." Winger swallowed and recovered. "I am glad that knowing Avish can help us now."

The companions sat and stared at the marks Wind-voice and Winger had drawn in the dirt. Could they truly be clues to the location of the sword?

"It's not much help, even if it *is* a clue," Stormac said at last. "Are you sure that's it, Wind-voice? I mean, you only got a glimpse of the thing."

"I—I *think* so," Wind-voice said doubtfully. But another memory was tugging at his mind. "There was a messenger. He said—he told the emperor that a knight, Sir Rattle-bones, would be bringing another gem from across the sea. A red one. He was carrying it then. He was supposed to be crossing the desert with it."

"The desert?" Fleydur said sharply, looking up. "The only way from the desert into the archaeopteryx territory is across the river that we just crossed."

The four of them looked at one another.

"I could go search for Rattle-bones," Wind-voice said. "If I could find him—if I could get that gem, maybe it would tell us something more about the hero's sword. Winger, can you teach me Avish? I've never had a chance to learn since I became a slave. I know learning things like this will help me in the future."

"Sure!" Winger said eagerly. "I'll come along and teach you as we go. Maybe you'll learn enough to read any clues that come our way."

"If there even *is* another clue," Stormac said skeptically. He shrugged. "The written old language makes my head ache. It's the type of thing that overlords care about, not common folk. Wielding a staff—that's the life for me."

"But if you learned Avish, no one could deceive you," Winger objected. He turned to the eagle.

"I'll come," Fleydur said. "You'll need me. I know the desert lands. I can help you search."

All three looked at Stormac. He scowled at them.

"I'm not even sure I believe all this," he grumbled. "Languages and clues! Legends and stories! We'd be better off doing something more practical. But . . . I'll come. We've *got* to fight against these archaeopteryxes somehow. I suppose a wild quest is no more than I deserve."

"Deserve?" Winger asked. Too late he noticed Windvoice shaking his head at him. The woodpecker had not seen the look of bitter shame on Stormac's face.

"What do you mean?" Wind-voice asked softly. "We're all victims of the archaeopteryxes, one way or another. Why should you deserve to suffer any more than we do?"

Stormac was silent. "You don't have to answer," Wind-voice said. "If you don't want to tell us . . ."

"No." Stormac sighed. "I'll tell you. I'm just afraid . . ." He picked up his staff in his claws and began to stroke the smooth wood. "Do you know of the Three Clans? The crows, the mynas, and the ravens? We stood out against the archaeopteryxes until our territory was over-run. We had two choices: flee into the wilderness or sur-render. Some of us made a bargain. In exchange for our lives and a scant measure of freedom, we'd serve in the archaeopteryx army. I . . . I left what remained of my own clan, after we'd starved for nearly a week, just for the promise of regular meals. I sold my allegiance for seed and worms, for strawberries and nuts. My job was sim-ply following the archaeopteryxes and carrying their supplies. No harm, I thought. How wrong I was."

Stormac's voice broke, and he took a deep breath. "Can I ever forgive myself, my foolish self?" he asked in a choked voice. "I followed the archaeopteryxes on my first mission. They overran a small village of swallows, trying to squeeze information regarding the gemstones' whereabouts out of them. Those little swallows fought so fiercely, but they had no chance, no chance at all. I never felt so much horror."

Stormac looked at Wind-voice. Wind-voice's face betrayed no emotion, but his eyes, shining out of his burned face, scared Stormac. They were so sunken, so dark, like black cherries dipped in ink; the steady, still gaze made him seem to be hunting for a hidden thing or perhaps just listening carefully. "I was like the fool who flew through a rain cloud, thinking it was cream, and came out wet on the other side. Now I wear this charm, this carving of a strawberry." Stormac gestured at the crude bit of red wood on a grass cord around his neck. "I will not be misled by food again, for I have my berry here. But . . . the harm I've done remains. I don't know if you can forgive me. If you want me on this search, I'll come. But since you know now what I've done . . ." Stormac's huge, watery eyes filled with despair. "If you want me to leave, I'll go."

"You don't have to go," Winger said gently. "Hard choices have been forced on us all, and sometimes we've made mistakes."

"He's right," said Fleydur. "What's passed is past."

They turned to look at Wind-voice, who gently put his claws over Stormac's.

"I don't have a real family or tribe anymore. But from the weeks we've been together, I know you are as close as a brother," said Wind-voice simply.

Fleydur led the way across the desert. They knew that Rattle-bones was heading northeast toward Castlewood, so they swung a little north in his direction. They scouted out dry canyons and looked through stands of dry, leafless scrub, hunting for signs of a traveling party of archaeopteryxes. Sometimes a cuckoo or a pygmy owl spoke to them of archaeopteryx sightings. They knew they were getting closer. As they camped each night, Winger drew figures in the sand and taught Wind-voice Avish by the light of the moon.

Then, on the fourth day, when they crossed the Amali River again—this time at a point up north, where it was only a quiet stream—they saw them. The four companions were traveling at the foot of a hill when Winger called out shrilly. The others looked up. There, just disappearing over the crest of the hill, with the sun shining on their backs, were the birds they sought: four archaeopteryxes, three garbed in light brown and the last in gray.

Wind-voice and his friends flew up the hill after them and slipped over the top to see the archaeopteryx band gliding down into a forested basin. The wind picked up the single gray cloak, and they saw a small package strapped onto the bird's back.

"Rattle-bones!" Ewingerale cried.

The bird suddenly spun around. "You'll be sorry to interfere with an archaeopteryx, you beggarbird of a musician!"

"Give us the package and we will not fight you," said Stormac.

"Ha! You wish, dinner-to-be!" The three other archaeopteryxes all whirled around, raising spears.

Wind-voice stared, eye-to-eye with Rattle-bones. Rattle-bones blinked and exclaimed, "You! 013-Unidentified, wanted on the poster!"

"There is no such bird," Wind-voice said.

The archaeopteryx threw a knife at Wind-voice. Then a bright flash of red light erupted from the package.

"What? The stone!" Rattle-bones shrieked.

When the light faded, the knife lay shattered on the ground, the leather pack beside it. Rattle-bones and the three other birds flapped their wings as hard as they could to get out of the vale.

Ewingerale picked up the leather bag. Stormac reached out a claw and lifted a flap.

Wind-voice saw something red glowing.

Winger picked up the gem gingerly and turned it over. On the other side was a shallow carving. The woodpecker brushed the feathers of one wing over it gently.

"Oh, the clue!" said Wind-voice eagerly.

Fleydur's head jerked up. He was looking at the crest of the hill where the archaeopteryxes had disappeared.

"I think perhaps we should think about the clue later," he said, staring hard at the sky. "I think—"

And then the others heard what he had: steady wing-beats thumping through the air.

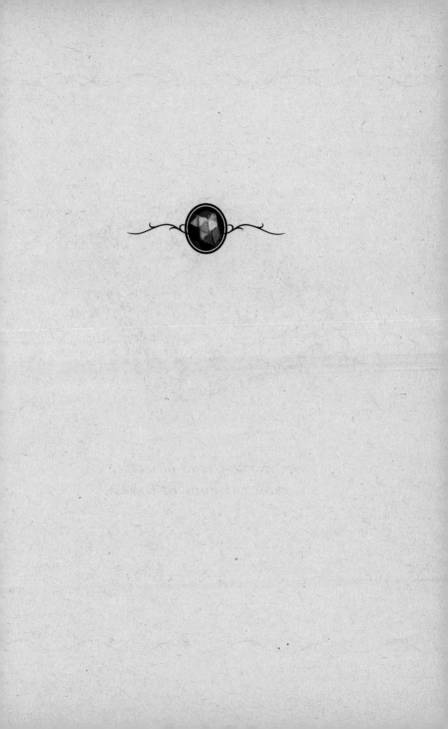

Archaeopteryxes are invincible!
—FROM THE *BOOK OF HERESY*

8

SCATTERED TO THE WINDS

The friends exchanged panicked looks.

"We can outrun them!" Winger cried.

"Too late," Fleydur said grimly. "Listen to that. There must be a hundred of them."

"Where did they come from?" Winger whispered.

Stormac shrugged and tossed his staff from claw to claw. "Who knows? They met an army regiment who were sent to receive them, maybe. How we're going to fight them is more important than where they came from."

"We need to distract them," Wind-voice said abruptly.

They came over the crest of the hill, an armed band of archaeopteryxes, swords flashing, maroon banners fluttering like ribbons of blood. Teeth glinted. Eyes flashed under leather headgear.

Rattle-bones was in the lead. "There they are!" His cry drifted to them faintly. "Seize them!"

"Ewingerale, keep the Leasorn safe and fly away!" Wind-voice shouted. "Quick! That new emperor can't get this gem. We can't let him know anything about the hero's sword! Fleydur, go with him!"

Fleydur flew with the woodpecker, slashing a path in the sky. Stormac drew his staff and planted himself back-to-back with Wind-voice.

Again and again Wind-voice brought down his sword, beating away the talons that raked at his eyes and clawed for his heart. He knew he and Stormac could not last more than a few minutes, but those minutes might be enough to let Winger and Fleydur escape.

A huge archaeopteryx came from behind the ranks and swung a cutlass that swept Wind-voice and Stormac apart. Gleefully, the large birds surged forward to fill the gap and keep them from each other. They were all laughing now.

Kawaka, Wind-voice realized with horror. *The big archaeopteryx is Kawaka. Oh, Stormac,* he thought sadly. He could not see the myna anymore. He opened both wings wide and whirled toward where he had last seen him. The archaeopteryxes in his vision blurred into a muddied sea. They backed away as his sword tip whisked about their faces, but not for long.

Wind-voice's blade smashed into Kawaka's helmet. It rang like a gong. His claws felt numb from the impact. He flew a little higher.

Kawaka cursed and roared a command. "That one— don't kill him! Take him alive!" A cudgel crashed full force between Wind-voice's shoulders, and he tumbled down. In a last attempt he spun again. The cutlass sought him and slashed across his back and chest.

Everything dimmed and swayed and he saw twisting colors. His wings faltered. He came to again as he fell on the ground, and he simply lay on his back on the blood-ied grass, staring through the layers of wings above him at a small patch of sky, a sky gray with despair.

They did not kill him. Instead, he was bound and blind-folded and dragged behind the soldiers to Castlewood.

"We have him," growled one of the archaeopteryxes, and at last the blindfold was removed. He was in a room.

An archaeopteryx pacing there stopped and turned. It was the head of the scholars.

His eyes flashed. "Where is it?" he demanded, swishing his sleeves left and right.

Wind-voice tried to look steady. "What do you mean?" His head felt too heavy for his body to hold upright.

The scholar seized the feathers on the back of Wind-voice's neck. "Where is it?" the archaeopteryx screeched. "Where is it? The gemstone in the sack! You had other birds fly away with it, didn't you? Where did they go? Don't pretend you don't know!"

"You won't get it anyhow." Wind-voice's sight went fuzzy.

"Tell me! Tell me!"

"No," gasped Wind-voice.

Then a smaller archaeopteryx scuttled in and spoke to the scholar, whose anger subsided at his words. He smoothed his robes. "The Ancient Wing shall see to you!"

Ewingerale and Fleydur huddled inside a hollow tree that had toppled onto its side, waiting to be sure all sounds of the archaeopteryxes' pursuit had faded away before they ventured out. The toothed birds had come close. A spear had actually been thrust through a knot-hole of the log where they were hiding and nicked one of Fleydur's flight feathers. But the soldiers had not found them and had moved on.

"What will Wind-voice and Stormac do?" Ewingerale clutched the bag, holding the gem to his chest.

"Let's hope for the best," the eagle murmured, unwilling to admit what he knew—that there was no hope. *Wind-voice and Stormac must be dead birds or prisoners by now.* "We must get this treasure to safety first. They would want that."

"Safety," muttered Winger. "Where can we find a place of safety? What about the healer, Rhea? Can she help us?"

Fleydur shook his head. "We can't ask her to take such a risk. The archaeopteryxes seem to want this gem badly. They will search everywhere nearby. If Rhea were caught with the stone . . ."

Winger shuddered. "How about just digging a hole and burying it? Or hiding it in a hollow tree?"

"You know how chaotic these times can be. We might not find it again."

"But then where?"

"I don't know." Fleydur's feathers drooped. "I can't . . . I can't think of a place. The archaeopteryxes are everywhere these days. I was supposed to keep you all safe from them, and I failed even in that. Perhaps there's no hope. There's nothing we can do."

Ewingerale gripped the red gemstone and was startled to see through his tears the eagle, who had so much more experience and had traveled so much farther, looking hopeless. He realized that this time it would be he, and not Fleydur, who would give the encouragement they needed.

"It's not the end," he cried.

Fleydur stared into the distance. Despite his size, despite his huge talons and sharp beak, he looked quite frail.

"It's only the beginning," Ewingerale insisted. "We still have something to hang on to. This Leasorn gem—we'll take it across the ocean. We'll take it to its home." Ewingerale, surprised, found himself the one making the plan, almost as if he were as strong as Fleydur, or as tough as Stormac, or as brave as Wind-voice. "And there's a clue." He turned the gleaming gemstone over. "'What you love most is the key.'"

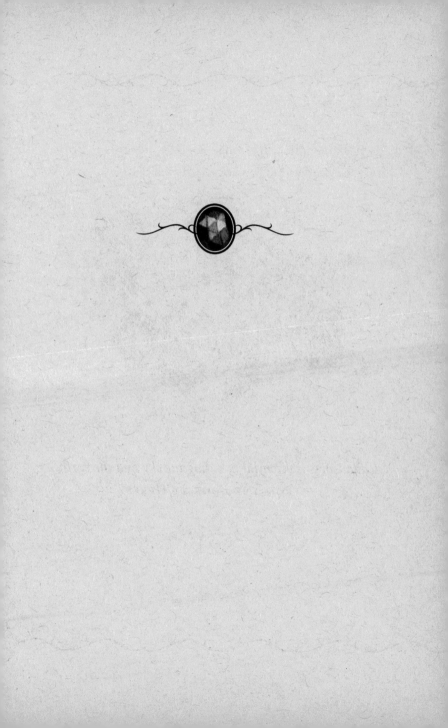

Callousness is essential to ruling the sky and the earth.
—FROM THE *BOOK OF HERESY*

9
A Bright Tale
of Darkness

Soldiers dragged Wind-voice along a hallway and thrust him into a small, private room. In a shadowy corner was the toucan, slumped inside a cage. Wind-voice was forced into a crouch on the ground, and then the soldiers were dismissed. Silence prevailed. Gradually, carefully, he raised his head. Wind-voice stared at Maldeor, and Maldeor let him stare, calmly unclasping his cloak and finishing a large, ripe pomegranate.

The onyx beak ring shone upon the gray bird's beak like a shard of glittering black ice, but it was Maldeor's left wing that held Wind-voice's gaze.

It was not a bird's wing at all. Up to his left shoulder, the feathers and skin looked normal enough, but then it merged with a bony limb and had a pale, gray, vaporous membrane, bare of feathers, stretched over it, spreading out like a huge fan. The limb, near the arch of the wing, had three talons with shiny claws, which Maldeor flexed. He grinned dourly at Wind-voice's gasp.

"Not pleasant, is it?" he asked, smiling a little. "But . . . effective."

How did he grow such a wing? thought Wind-voice. *Can he still fly?*

Maldeor raised and lowered the grotesque wing. Then, as if losing interest, he folded it onto his back.

"You have suffered much, I think," he said, looking thoughtfully at Wind-voice. The white bird was surprised to hear something that might have been sympathy in his voice. "From my court I have heard that you showed defiance in old Hungrias's face. I like that; he deserved more birds treating him that way. Yet he tried to burn you on a fire, didn't he? That old toadstool! It must have been terrible . . . but I know what pain is like. The most worthy birds can turn suffering into strength.

My mentor has taught me that. Are you that strong, I wonder?"

Maldeor lowered his heavy lids and sighed. For a moment, Wind-voice thought that the archaeopteryx emperor, despite his wry and tired face, was lonely. But the illusion faded.

Maldeor sliced another pomegranate open with a sudden jerk, using a talon on his left wing. Red juice spattered about, and the seeds tumbled out like rubies at his feet. "Weak birds have no right to live. Weak, ignorant, foolish, selfish birds—I have gained this throne to put an end to their evil. But I need a weapon to do so. I'm close to finding it already. But I think you may know something about it, since you were so interested in that gem. So perhaps you are able to help me."

"Waterways . . . birds live near waterways . . ." Stormac was panting, flying as hard as he could through torrents of rain, following the path of the river that ran through Castlewood.

He tried not to think but to focus all his energy on seeking some movements of birds in the trees on each bank. Trickles of blood dripped down his chest, mixing with the rain. His berry pendant swung to and fro. He must fly faster . . . faster . . . The archaeopteryxes had taken Wind-voice toward Castlewood. But Stormac knew he could do little against them on his own. He needed help.

He glimpsed a flash of red and blue in a great grove of trees far down the south bank. "Hey there!" he croaked over the roar of the river. "Help me!"

His overworked wings were throbbing and he coughed out rainwater, but relief swept through him as he neared and saw that the birds he had seen were macaws, known for their resistance to the archaeopteryxes. "Help. I really need help," he gasped. "My friend and I were attacked by archaeopteryxes in the desert. I managed to survive, but—" He landed on a branch, and his vision blurred as tears oozed out of his eyes. He blinked rapidly. "Please, can you help me find him? Maybe he is still alive . . ." Then, to his astonishment and disappointment, his legs wobbled under him and he slumped onto his perch, his wings hanging by his sides.

The two macaws talked briefly together in low, muttering tones and then came forward to carry Stormac between them. "My friends, please," he mumbled, but he was too weak to object as they took him to a clearing in the woods. A small fire was burning in a ring of stones under the shelter of a tree whose thick branches were interwoven with vines to keep the rain out. They laid

Stormac down near it.

A medicine bird stepped forward and offered him a cup of warm herbal brew. "I am Kari," she said. "A long way you've come. What brings you here, friend?"

So Stormac, reviving a little, told her and the macaws of the legends of the hero, the herons' amber, Rattlebones and the red Leasorn, and the battle.

" . . . I don't know, but clang, clang, clang, and I lost sight of Wind-voice, feathers and all," he said. "I was trying to fight my way back to him when a warrior with a morning star struck me and sent me sailing into a tiny crack between two boulders. I went out like a candle. The crack was too small for them to fit in, thank the Great Spirit! I must have looked quite dead. I guess they jabbed at me with their longest weapons and hooked out some of my chest feathers as a trophy . . ." Stormac trailed off. "All this, for a gemstone!"

"The gemstone was worth it," Kari said sternly.

Stormac knew he owed the macaws a great deal, but he felt his anger rising. "Worth my friend's life?" he demanded.

Kari didn't answer directly. "You said the heron's yellow gemstone has carvings on one of its facets," she remarked. "And you think the red one is probably like it."

The myna nodded.

"Well," she continued, "we have a gem of our own. It is a great treasure of our tribe. There is a clue written on it—"

"Clues! Heroes! I don't care! The gemstones themselves are lovely enough, but I place life before fables." Stormac's face was stricken. "Wind-voice, that young fellow . . . he had such a keen interest in them, more than the rest of us, and now whether he's dead or alive I don't know!"

"But you kept the red stone away from the emperor, even if you don't believe in the story of the gems," Kari insisted. "For that we are in your debt. We'll send birds to search for your friend and help you all we can; for now, you must rest."

Fleydur grew strangely still, as if listening to an echo of Winger's words. *What you love most is the key.*

"Love," he murmured. He ruffled his feathers in a flustered manner, paused, and repeated, "Love." He glanced at Ewingerale, agitated. "I wonder," he said, "if those clues are not just clues to help the hero find the sword but words of wisdom. If it hadn't been for love, I wouldn't have been so happy once, and so unhappy now. If it hadn't been for love, I would not have been in bells and beads, with song and dance . . ."

"You told us that you're an orphan from the Skythunder Mountains . . . but you aren't," Ewingerale said.

Fleydur reached out a claw and touched the Leasorn. "No. I'm not an orphan, but I have no family. Once I was a prince; strange, isn't it, Winger? I was a son of Morgan, the chieftain of the eagles. My brother, Forlath, and I were kept in our mountains by our elders. Seeing our size and number, the archaeopteryxes did not trouble us mountain folk. They expanded their lands everywhere else, but they stopped at our foothills.

"You know how youngsters are; I was curious. I'd seen archaeopteryxes, but I knew there were more things out there as well, more kinds of birds. But as the eldest son of the leader, I was expected to be perfect: brave, stalwart, familiar with every event in our history and each bygone battle; good with a sword, with military strategies, and fancy flying skills for display. I wasn't supposed to be filling my head with dreams about the world beyond the mountains."

"Your family loved you," Ewingerale said.

"Yes, and I loved them, too. But one day when a woodland sparrow from beyond came and told stories of misfortune and terror . . . I changed. She was a musician, too. She played a reed flute."

Ewingerale understood. "Then you loved music."

"Did I! It was such a heartwarming thing. I'd secretly hum melodies in the valleys when nobird was around. Eagles don't sing, you know—not really—and music was supposed to be beneath the dignity of a prince. But from then on I was distracted, thinking of songs. I learned my sword well enough, and knew enough flying tricks to last me quite a while, but as I listened to my tutor's lessons on this or that long-dead bird's history and deeds to make the tribe safer and better, I couldn't help thinking, Certainly this is important, but this is the past. What about all those suffering birds out there, in the forests and flatlands beyond our mountain stronghold?

"On the other hand, Forlath was everything I couldn't be. He was perfect—wonderfully so—and I felt that nobird would miss me if I went, for he would be a much better leader than I would be.

"And so, one night after a lesson on history, I slipped

away down the mountains. I had not flown far when I found a campfire. The poor souls there! They let me join them and offered to share their bread and beetles. It could not be compared to the feast of river mussels and fish with pine seeds that had been spread on the table at my home, but it was all they had, and they shared it willingly. I told them I would sing in return for what they gave me. Oh, but Great Spirit, Winger! The poor fellows seemed to be in another world, so happy. Their eyes seemed to be cleared of doubt and worry. When I left them, they looked stronger. I was dazed as I reached home, and my father stormed out with many of the elders of my tribe. He'd suspected for some time that my heart was elsewhere. He'd sent a bird to spy on me when I left, and that bird had reported back everything I had done.

"He was furious. 'We put so much hope in you, Fleydur,' he said. 'You have disappointed me.' He told me that this would be my last day at home. 'Do you care so much for others, and place them before your own tribe? Singing, for all the world, like a beggar! It's beneath you. Go, then. Go to your starving friends and throw your dignity to the winds. You are not my son anymore. I only have Forlath. Leave!'

"I was disowned and exiled from my home. My love

for my family clashed with my love for music and my love for others. I—I don't know why they would think that singing was lowly . . . These ages are truly dark. Yet the power of music never changes. It"—Fleydur's eyes shone—"is mighty. Swords and even words can disturb or hurt, but music's strength is to heal. To bring life, hope, and joy."

Fleydur turned away. "I think we come to this world to have a happy life. Treasure and social rank—these are just external things. You can't take them with you to your grave. Those decadent clan customs that place value on material things above all else can imprison our minds. I'm glad that I was able to break away from them and drift all around the earth, singing to everybird."

Ewingerale listened with sympathy.

"I don't regret my decision . . ." Fleydur murmured. He carefully wrapped the red gemstone in a linen cloth and placed it inside his knapsack. "But . . . I miss my family. I truly do . . ."

"With Wind-voice and Stormac gone, you are the closest I have to a family, Winger." He stood up, shuddering. "Crossing a whole ocean! The very thought makes me feel seasick already. Golden eagles aren't built for saltwater; ospreys are." He winked at Winger. "Who would have thought that a woodpecker would attempt such a thing too? But"—Fleydur chuckled—"I guess it's high time for the world to turn upside down. We should get going if we're to reach the seaside before the sun sets."

Both birds cautiously made their way out of the hollow log. Ewingerale flew up and looked back one last time to see if maybe, just maybe, Wind-voice and Stormac might appear.

"Fleydur!" he screamed. "Quick, archaeopteryxes! They're still searching for us!"

Nobility could be embodied in one shining act.

—FROM THE OLD SCRIPTURE

10
A NEW TURN

There they were: Two young birds in a castle, staring at each other, pale eyes into black, an archaeopteryx and an unidentifiable bird, one reclining upon a whalebone perch and the other crouched on the floor, one waiting and the other resting.

"No," Wind-voice replied at last. Maldeor's batlike wing somehow reminded him of Yin Soul. "I will not help you."

The spark in the white bird's eyes clouded Maldeor's vision so that a shimmering image of the dove Irene surfaced from his memory. *Why didn't I notice that before?* thought Maldeor. A foul taste rose in his beak.

Then a soldier hurried in, holding a clump of bloodied black feathers, and saluted. Maldeor did not look up.

Wind-voice swallowed his gasp—the feathers had that familiar purple gloss. They were Stormac's.

"Good. Go join your friend in Sky Land." Ignoring the soldier, the Ancient Wing jumped from his throne and struck Wind-voice's neck with his left wing. His claws sank into flesh.

I won't cry in front of Maldeor, Wind-voice thought, throbbing with pain.

"Your eyes will rot," Maldeor's grip tightened. "The dark magic of my wing will rot them. You cursed crossbreed and your lot, always wrecking my plans." He thrust Wind-voice at his soldiers. "You're too lowly for me to kill. But don't worry. You'll still die in agony."

All the while, Ozzan, the blacksmith toucan, watched through a swollen, blue-lidded eye. He felt that the white bird was quite brave to stand up to Maldeor. He himself had been tortured in all manners imaginable. They beat him, they hung him upside down by his feet, and they poured chili pepper oil onto his face. Last night a sleeping draught had been forced on him. He had tried to clamp his beak closed, but in the end the potion had trickled down his throat and he had slept. Unknowingly, he must have murmured in his sleep about Kauria, about Pepheroh, and about the sword. He knew this because later, when he had woken, Maldeor had jeered in his face and thanked him in his sarcastic gracious manner for what he had revealed. What if Maldeor really captured the sword!

Somehow, Ozzan's heavy heart felt lighter as he watched Wind-voice.

That evening, as the rain stopped and the sky turned red, Wind-voice was marched out to a log and chained to it. More soldiers came, dragging the faltering toucan. Wind-voice's vision had worsened. He could barely make out the bird's closed eyes and a bleeding whip mark that had nearly cut his face in half. The toucan did not struggle in the least as he was tied next to Wind-voice along the log; he simply laid his huge beak to one side. Maldeor watched, motionless, as his soldiers lifted the log and plopped it into the river.

Neither prisoner spoke as the log drifted slowly. Very soon their feathers were wet all the way through.

However, at the moment the archaeopteryxes were out of sight, the blacksmith grew animated and started to gnaw at Wind-voice's rusty chains. Whenever the log bobbed and turned, one of them held his breath as he was submerged in the water, but the toucan did not bother to stop his work.

"Why are you trying to free me and not yourself?" Wind-voice gasped to the blur of black and yellow.

"You must be free. You must."

Rocks began to appear, jutting out of the river and slicing the water like knives. Every time their log hit one, they spun in treacherous circles. Then the current picked up speed, and Wind-voice felt as if the water had washed away all his thoughts. There was a roar in the distance, the sound not of a battle, as he thought at first, but of a waterfall.

"Free yourself while there is time!" Wind-voice cried.

The toucan shook his head. "Don't worry about me. It doesn't matter anymore. Maldeor seeks the sword, the one from my homeland, Kauria . . . " His eyes clouded with shame. He rasped on: "I told things, under torture and the effects of a sleeping potion. I don't know how much I spoke. . . . But you—I can feel it, looking in your eyes—you can still stop him."

The rushing sound came nearer, nearer.

"No! A few seconds more, a few seconds more . . ." Ozzan's beak had worn away a tiny slash in the dull iron, but the link still held firm. In his desperation he spat out the chain and rammed at it with the tip of his beak.

The log shot forward. A rush of air gushed all around them. Below came the terrible roar.

"Stop Maldeor!" Ozzan croaked. Using the last ounce of his life strength, he reared his powerful old neck back and brought his beak down on the chains that bound Wind-voice just as he used to beat iron on his anvil. Only this time he was not forging metal but forging hope.

Ewingerale pulled the dark hood of his vest over his bright red head.

"They haven't noticed us yet," Fleydur said grimly. He pulled off his bells, muffled them quickly in a wad of moss, and put them into his knapsack. Together the eagle and the woodpecker put distance behind them as they skirted the desert and bore on toward the lands of the Forests Battalion.

The dry, stony land slowly turned green, and they glimpsed a river in the distance. As they crossed the river, the ground gave away to a shaded valley waving with bracken. A rocky hill rose in the distance. Fleydur soared higher into the air and called for Ewingerale to cling to his back. A tailwind carrying the sounds of rattling yelps told them that they had been spotted by the archaeopteryxes, but Fleydur didn't seem the least bit worried.

When he was above the rocky hill, he snagged a thermal updraft and, spreading his wings so that all of the primary feathers at his wing tips were separated, spiraled high into the sky. The archaeopteryxes below, yammering away, flapped furiously in pursuit, but their crooked wings could not catch the wind as well as Fleydur's did, and their tails were heavy. They were not built for long, soaring flights. Fleydur grinned as arrows and spears shot at them by the archaeopteryxes fell harmlessly back to earth. Ewingerale was struck silent by the beauty of the vastness, high in the crystal cloudless sky, where their only companion, apart from each other, was the sun.

More powerful winds that existed only at high altitudes carried them along, and, selecting a quick gust that bore them briskly seaward, they flew onward, chasing the sun. The great golden ball flushed red in anger at this pursuit and sank faster.

As evening bore on, Ewingerale and Fleydur saw a slice of something glittering along the horizon. Above them, the sky bled through banners of stratocumulus clouds. All of a sudden they soared over a fringe of pale white beach that clung to a shore, and then the sea welled up, worried and wrinkled, beneath them. The two shadows that they cast onto its surface were pounded to pieces by the waves.

When the sun finally drowned in the ocean, the stars flickered to life.

It would take five days and nights of continuous flying before they reached the other shore. When they arrived, they would be surprised at the sight of the White Cap Mountains.

When they arrived, they would be surprised that the Waterthorn tribe was waiting for them.

When they arrived, they would be even more surprised at what the robins had to say.

One of the hardest things to break is the tie of family.
—FROM THE OLD SCRIPTURE

11

THE GREEN GEM
AND THE PURPLE GEM

ind-voice's mind was taking him on strange flights. In his imagination, he saw heavy eyelids hiding tortured yet triumphant eyes, the slight nod of a familiar head, that sincere, dangerous, glittering smile.

And he saw again, with a cold rush of air into his very bones, Yin Soul, waiting, against a background of candle-studded rocks and leaping flames. Had Yin Soul offered Maldeor the same thing he had offered Wind-voice? Was that what the archaeopteryx had meant when he spoke of his mentor? When nobody understood or cared for Maldeor, had Yin Soul pretended to, and seized him?

Wind-voice's eyes slowly opened and he sat up. His vision was even worse. The evil magic from Maldeor's batlike wing was working. "The toucan . . . the black-smith . . . I have to thank him; he broke my chains—"

He saw a dark blur, and a voice came from that direction. "The poor bird's dead. I don't know where Fleydur and Ewingerale are. Wind-voice, what did they do to you?"

"Wanted me to help him . . . the Ancient Wing, the new one, not Hungrias. He believes in our legend of the hero. He knows about the sword." Wind-voice paused as a headache drummed on the inside of his skull. "And the legend, more than ever, is real. That toucan, he is a black-smith of Kauria . . ." *He died, but he saved me,* Wind-voice thought, and tears fell from his eyes, clouding his vision even more.

"What? Maldeor seeks it?" a new voice shouted, drip-ping with horror. Wind-voice looked toward a blur of brilliant red.

"That's Kari," a dark bird whispered in his ear.

Wind-voice blinked hard to clear his vision. "Stormac? They said—I thought you were dead! How did you find me?"

"I was sure you had gone to Sky Land too," Stormac said, perching near Wind-voice's bed of cushiony grass. "But I found the parrots, and they helped me search for you. We discovered you, flung onto the grass on the bank, the body of that poor toucan swirling in the pool at the bottom of the waterfall."

Kari, however, was incensed to hear of Maldeor's plan. "Dead? We'll all be shining bones, soon enough, with Maldeor! How could he be still alive? I never thought Maldeor knew about the sword!" Kari's voice rose above the scream of cicadas around them. "Do you know if he's found any of the remaining Leasorn gems?"

"The yellow gemstone of the kingfishers," Stormac said, thinking back. "He must have that one. But we kept the red Leasorn gem from him. I don't think he has any more."

Wind-voice was intrigued, however. "*Remaining* Leasorn gems? What do you mean?"

"I thought you knew. You must know." Kari's eyes were round. "But no—it happened two years ago. There was one gemstone, more famous than the other ones because the Avish words on it were not a riddle at all. It was with a tribe of doves, and it told of Hero's Day. Surely you've heard of that . . . it's next spring."

Wind-voice tried hard to focus on Kari. *My mother is a dove!* he thought.

"The tribesbirds were nearly all slaughtered by Maldeor and his soldiers; the gem somehow disappeared. He lost Prince Phaëthon, too. That was why Hungrias punished him."

"Do you think that's why Maldeor hates me?" Wind-voice asked.

Nobird knew what to say.

Kari continued, "We know the archaeopteryxes wanted the Leasorn simply because Hungrias likes beautiful gems. Now I suspect Maldeor knows about the hero's sword. Birdkind is in even greater peril. He'll be crazed looking for it, and with his army he will be unstoppable." Kari sighed. "At least the green Leasorn is safe for now."

Kari cupped something in her claws. They all leaned toward it. Wind-voice tried to squint through his still-fuzzy vision. To his surprise it cleared, and he saw that it was a stone she held, and in that stone were two figures flying over something vast—perhaps it was an illusion. Then he blinked, and miraculously his vision was restored.

"Peace opens the door," Wind-voice read excitedly,

tracing a claw over the carvings on the gem.

"We parrots and macaws feel sad," Kari said. "We live so long, and so we witness far more cruelty. Before the archaeopteryxes, four-winged dinosaurs plagued us. Will these times ever end? Our gem itself seems to have some magic. It can help heal the wounds of birds who go near it."

It healed Maldeor's dark magic, Wind-voice thought, awed.

". . . But it is too feeble to heal all the troubles of our times, when thousands of birds all over the territories hurt each day. 'Peace opens the door.' Whatever it means, I wonder, when will peace come?"

Nobird spoke for a while, and then Stormac grumbled, "I don't believe this. Besides, what use are these clues? Nobird can understand them!"

Wind-voice ignored the question. "Sooner or later, I must start off again. I don't know where Ewingerale and Fleydur are . . . but will you come with me, Stormac?"

"Yes, of course. We can make our way back to Fisher and the herons."

"No, we can't." Wind-voice's voice was low. "We have to find more of these stones."

"What?" The myna exploded. "Lore, legend, myth. Dealing with these foolish things brings nothing but trouble. I care about *now*. For our lives and futures. If these special gemstones grew like a bunch of grapes on a vine, then fine. But they don't!" He pounded the floor with his staff. "How in the world are you going to find another one? Let me guess: Wander around like a beggar-bird, with the archaeopteryxes on your tailfeathers? You are going mad, aren't you?"

A silence followed. Wind-voice stared into Stormac's bright brown eyes. Then the myna looked away. Wind-voice looked down at the green gemstone and saw his own reflection: Partway into a molt, he had bald patches and uneven sprouts of new feathers among his splotchy, burnt feathers. Bumps on his head. Scabs. Bloodshot eyes. Yes, he looked nothing short of mad.

A memory of Fleydur's voice, something the eagle had mentioned, came to him. He raised his eyes and whispered, "Skythunder . . ."

Morgan, the eagle chieftain who once had been able to smash rock into dust, was terribly ill.

Many thought it was the worries of leadership, the

tension of watching the archaeopteryxes expand their territory, that had made him fall sick. Medicine birds were called, and they checked his tongue and looked at his eyes. They gave him dandelion tea, fresh herbs, dry herbs, hairy ones, pungent ones. But no matter what medicine Morgan took or how much he rested, he grew steadily worse.

Only Forlath knew that his father was heartsick for his eldest son.

Morgan had tried to push thoughts of the headstrong young eagle out of his mind since he had disowned him. Yet his grief gnawed at his heart.

"They don't call these mountains Skythunder for nothing," Stormac said, awed. Wind-voice and Stormac, after weeks of recovery and rest, had set out for the homeland of Fleydur.

Each peak loomed up to greet them. Delicate wisps of purple mist crowned the ledges. The slopes were sleek with ferns and violets, and pine trees linked branches as they hailed the sky.

When the two companions reached the foothills, an eagle swooped down from a high ledge, screaming, "Who are you? If you seek passage to the tundra beyond the mountains, follow that stream. It will lead you to a pass through the mountain range. Other than that, no strangers are allowed here!"

"We do not seek passage," Wind-voice said clearly. "We wish to find Morgan, king of the eagles."

"If you are sent here to represent the archaeopteryx empire, the chief wishes you well, but he cannot see you at present," said the eagle wearily.

"No, we come in the name of Fleydur, a bird of the Skythunder tribe," Wind-voice answered.

"We do not know him." The eagle landed on a dead pine tree. He shifted his weight from one set of talons to the other, so the branch shook. Stormac looked at Wind-voice, confused.

The sentry eagle turned and let out a series of short screams. Another eagle, larger, somehow familiar, swung into view. He landed on the same branch, and his gaze pierced the two travelers.

Then, though it almost broke his heart, Forlath said quite slowly and deliberately, "There is no Fleydur."

"That's ridiculous!" Stormac burst out. "We met him, we know him, we fought alongside him!"

Forlath shook his head again. "The bird that you name—he does not exist."

Wind-voice froze and then tried again. "Well, whoever our friend was, we shared many a song together. I think he would like us to give you a gift, like gifts he always gives to birds around him."

Forlath's heart was racing. It took all his training in dignity and courtesy to stop happy tears from spilling out of his great brown eyes.

"It is something that thousands of birds would like, something that some birds would even die for," Wind-voice murmured. Stormac shot him a worried glance. He smiled reassuringly and continued. "Its luster outshines the best of diamonds; its durability is greater than iron or stone. It is so valuable that nobird has ever dared to place a price upon it. The most precious thing in the world!" He placed his claws in the feathers over his heart and reached out, his claws closed over something. He uncurled them slowly.

"Love." He smiled gently over his empty, open claws.

"He still loves us! Oh, Fleydur, my brother," Forlath said, his face collapsing in a confusion of sadness and joy. The mask of dignity faded, and Wind-voice found himself looking at the same kind eyes that he remembered from Fleydur's face.

"Come, do come. Tell me more of the elder brother of mine. I haven't seen him for so many seasons." The eagle prince led them to Sword Mountain, the highest peak in the range.

Morgan, the eagle king, was astounded when his son, Forlath, laughing and crying, brought in a myna and a strange white bird, and was even more so when he heard of their adventures with archaeopteryxes and gemstones and with Fleydur. He sat up straighter on his perch, and a wrinkle in his heart softened.

For the first time that day, the old eagle spoke. "Yes, indeed, we have a gem, like the macaws, the robins, and the herons. It is purple, like our mountains." He gestured, and Forlath brought out a chest. The eagle prince opened it, and the stone within seemed to be the embodiment of majestic pride and dignity.

"And see here," Morgan continued, tracing a talon over a carving. "The Avish script."

"'Look into the eyes to choose your path,'" Wind-voice read carefully.

"That's right!" Morgan exclaimed, looking glad and surprised that another bird recognized Avish. "Whatever it means, though, I don't know. But I know one thing." Morgan closed his eyes, and then he opened them again to look at Wind-voice. "Perhaps it's time for a change. You tell me of troubles, of war, of darkness, of tyranny. I was wrong to merely watch and do nothing, to forbid our youngsters to go out into danger. If the tale of the hero's sword is true and this new emperor, Maldeor, can lay his claws upon it . . ." He looked at Forlath. "There are many things that I've done that I regret, things I believed were for the best. I hope we can still help." He nodded. "Yes, it is time to let the world know what our standards are. We value family. We defend one another, and without a doubt it can be said that the birds out there, suffering, are our family too!"

"Aye!" Forlath was grinning widely.

"Wind-voice, Stormac," the chieftain said, "I wish you

the best of luck. Maldeor indeed must be stopped. I know one thing that may help you: There are gemstones in the south."

Forlath turned to Stormac. "My father is not yet well, so I will help you. I will fly the range, gather forces far and wide, and amass an army. We shall meet you in the frigid seas." He dipped his golden head. "One warrior's promise to another."

And so, as Forlath departed to gather allies, Windvoice and Stormac set off for the loneliest, coldest lands.

The eagle chieftain's health grew better day after day, and it was not long before he was spotted flying alone, slowly, to the tallest pine on Sword Mountain. Gazing at the starry night sky, he took a deep breath.

"Fleydur . . ." His old voice crackled as he cried to the wind. "Fleydur, your father misses you . . ."

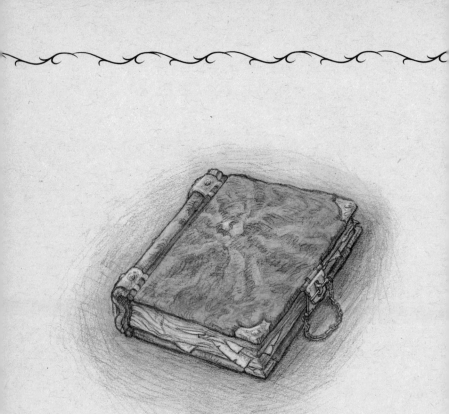

We who are alive have no idea how desperately the dead struggle to come back to the mortal world.
—FROM THE *BOOK OF HERESY*

12
THE LAST DEAL

The dried claws, gripping a piece of charcoal, added a stain to the queue of tallies on the stone wall above the mantle. He counted silently. "No!" The charcoal fell from his claws.

For Yin Soul, time was measured in months, until today. After their first meeting, Maldeor had had to come to him at the end of every month to drink a potion that infused power into Yin Soul's magical wing.

How Yin Soul flattered and soothed Maldeor at each meeting, advising the archaeopteryx of his quest! Yin Soul needed time to ensure that he would win Maldeor's trust completely. *If only I had been more careful with 013-Unidentified! That bird, with his honesty, would have been a better victim.* He regretted his folly, especially when he discovered from Maldeor that 013-Unidentified was also seeking the gemstones.

Yin Soul's claws closed into fists. If he had had a heart still, it would have writhed in his chest like a slimy, dying grub. *Just a week, just a week!* Only a week till his pending destruction: the day of the arrival of a hero. "I must live, live, live . . . !" Yin Soul strode back and forth across his room looking wildly around, snatching books out of his high shelves. Then, with a distracted howl, he tossed them aside. No books could save him now from his doom, but Maldeor could.

"If he would agree to swallow my essence!" Yin Soul talked rapidly to himself, his voice growing shriller by the second. "If he would swallow it! Maldeor, Maldeor! Oh, tricky, evil, scheming Maldeor! Once I am inside your body, your soul will gradually die, you hateful bird . . . but I need you. Savior and fool, come! Come! Yes, he must save me. He will!" Yin Soul's voice crackled like thunder.

Then there was an echoing noise. Startled, like a tiny sparrow in the shadow of a hawk, Yin Soul froze and fell silent. His hunchbacked figure cast a crooked shadow on the bookshelves. The noise came again, louder and more insistent now:

Caw! Caw! Caw!

"He comes, he comes," Yin Soul muttered solemnly, rubbing his forelimbs slowly together as he prepared for the last deal—the ultimate trick, the meanest lie.

He closed his shriveled eyelids. He stood straight as the wind from the raven messenger fluttered his manteau. He waited for the thump of something dropped onto his carpet, and only then did he slowly turn around.

"Greetings, Maldeor."

Maldeor picked himself up from his fall. "Mentor, normally the wing potion gives me strength for a month of flying. Why am I here when only four days have passed?"

"You must have worked hard, Maldeor, following your quest and ruling your empire at the same time. Ah, it must have put strain upon the magic of the potion . . . But toiling so hard, you have found many clues, have you not?" Yin Soul tucked the claws of his forewings into his manteau and inclined his head.

"Of course!" Maldeor said crisply. "One clue I found

from actual gemstones; one from you, Mentor, about Hero's Day. I learned more from a foolish toucan from Kauria." His face glowed with venomous pleasure.

"But do you have them all?"

Maldeor's pale eyes turned brittle. "I have something better than gems—I know where Kauria itself is." He leaned forward. "Give me the wing potion. I must depart for Kauria, and the flight will be a hard one."

Yin Soul picked up the skull of a bird. In it sloshed the

silvery draft. Maldeor almost snatched it, he took it so fast. Head bent, he stretched out a leathery, freckled tongue and violently started lapping up the magic potion.

"You don't, do you!" Yin Soul advanced toward the archaeopteryx. Maldeor stopped drinking. "You don't have all the clues to the sword." Yin Soul shook his head. "What are you going to do about that, Maldeor, eh? It would be a pity, getting so close, you know, so close! Then, losing it all."

The archaeopteryx finished his draft. "Are you saying that I'm a foolish hatchling with half an eggshell over my head? My wits are enough to cover the clues I don't have!" He was smiling dangerously, his eyes forming into triangular slits.

"You are clever, little emperor, but do you want to risk losing the sword?"

Maldeor flipped his bloodshot eyes up to Yin Soul. "No," he said slowly. "What else can I do?"

It is time! I shall return to the living world soon! Yin Soul thought. "Remember, Maldeor? Remember when I first met you and gave you your wing, I said that I would have an even better deal for you?"

"Yes!"

"Well, what do you think of the wing? Isn't it fine?

This deal would outshine it. Do you want it?"

"Yes, do tell me, Mentor." Maldeor whispered fervently.

Yin Soul turned aside so that shadows veiled his face. He took a plate from his desk. *He must! He must accept this. He will!* He opened his beak, strings of shiny saliva sticking to his teeth. His eyes rolled backward and he started coughing vigorously, the veins popping up in his neck, and making nasal noises that echoed in the room.

He made one last great whoop, and something slid slowly out of his beak and splattered onto the plate he was holding.

Then Yin Soul wiped his beak with a sleeve. He turned to face Maldeor, who had gone pale beneath his feathers.

"Drink it! Drink it heartily!" He held the plate under Maldeor's beak.

Maldeor felt his own throat contract. An awful smell of rotting flesh triggered an urge to vomit, so he didn't dare to open his beak. His gaze fastened onto the contents of the plate: What was that generous dollop of something the color of liver—dull brownish purple, flecked with swirls of gray and slightly steaming?

Disgust almost overwhelmed him. "What is it? What will it do?"

"Maldeor—oh, Maldeor, if you swallow it"—Yin Soul's voice was getting higher—"your wing will never need a potion again! Never, I promise you!"

"Really?" That was something. Maldeor's beak moved a little closer toward the thick slime.

"Yes, and if you drink it, you will most definitely get the sword. I assure you, you shall be a hero!" Yin Soul could hardly conceal the feverishness in his voice.

Maldeor was elated. Yin Soul watched with equal rapture as the archaeopteryx held the plate and made a motion as if to scoop the purple goo into his open beak. Then suddenly the archaeopteryx stopped. Yin Soul's smile wavered.

"You still haven't told me what this is," Maldeor said. His eyes flashed as realization dawned upon him.

Yin Soul watched, twitching, wanting to shout, *No!*

"Nothing is ever free in this world," Maldeor whispered. "Why—"

"I want to help you, guide you, my dear pupil!" Yin Soul gushed. "Give you chances, watch you grow! If you drink it, I will be with you, inside your body. I have skill!"

Maldeor started to put the plate down.

"No, Maldeor—oh, you don't know. You will make wrong choices without me; you will fall into traps. You stand little chance of getting the sword!"

"I don't need you stuck to me like some leech. So you want to share the glory with me? I alone shall be the hero. I've proven that already. What do you know? I can get the sword, and I will!" Maldeor tossed the plate aside. It shattered against the stone wall. Yin Soul bolted to retrieve his essence. The way Yin Soul ran struck Maldeor as somewhat familiar. He gasped in surprise when Yin Soul tripped on his own sash and the manteau came apart. One leg was a wooden peg. The other was like a wing.

Scenes flashed before Maldeor's eyes—the battle with the dove tribe, the gemstone in the prince's claws, the monster leaping out. More scenes came, faster and faster, till his vision was nearly blinded, stamped with the blurring profile of the four-winged dinosaur. "You! You are that winged creature!" Maldeor's roar was pure horror and hatred. He could almost hear again the royal prosecutor proclaiming him a criminal, then the chop and thud of the scythe, the crack of bone and the hiss as blood spurted out, the *plop* when his severed wing fell onto the dust. He could almost feel again that pain.

Yin Soul scrambled over, turning his head in all directions like a madbird. "No, I'm not! Please!" he howled. "Please, Maldeor!" He crouched at the archaeopteryx's feet, claws holding tight to Maldeor's leg. Again and again he kowtowed, sobbing. In his forewing he held his stinky, jelly-like essence upward toward Maldeor beseechingly.

"Get off!" Maldeor kicked Yin Soul.

"No, Maldeor . . . I gave you a wing . . . I gave you power!"

"If it hadn't been for you, I would never have been stripped of my rank, accused of treason! I would have never been de-winged! I would have never been cast out! All my troubles were because of you. I deserve this new wing. You gave me nothing! I owe you nothing!" Maldeor yelled for the raven to take him out.

"What are you talking about? There are so many of my kind out there . . . you must have mistaken me for another creature! No, don't leave me . . . You can't . . ." Yin Soul gasped. His eyes peered up at Maldeor. Tears were streaming down Yin Soul's face, real ones this time.

The raven messenger beat his wings and hovered about Maldeor, who jumped up and grabbed his feet. They started to rise. Yin Soul fumbled with his torn sash and drew out a magical knife capable of separating a body from a spirit. Grunting, he rose into the air and slashed at Maldeor. Feathers floated to the ground. When he finally managed to get the blade against Maldeor's throat, he hesitated. *He is my last hope . . .*

In that moment of hesitation, the raven and Maldeor rose out of Yin Soul's prison. Yin Soul's knife dropped to the ground. He fluttered up as high as he could go in the confines of his dwelling, his face a wrinkled contortion of pain as he screamed and pounded madly on the walls—*boom, boom, boom!* His eyes desperate and shining brightly, he flung out his crooked forewing at Maldeor's disappearing figure.

"Your wing shall not last you across the ocean! You will come back tomorrow! YOU WILL!"

Everything is ready. Provisions are packed, soldiers fed and trained, clues studied—so why am I still nervous? Only six more days left. One hundred and forty-four hours . . . How many of those hours are to be spent flying over a tossing ocean? The magic wing was already jerking in spasms. *Curse Yin Soul . . . but I'm not flying! I've already arranged for a sky carriage to be built just last evening when I came back from Yin Soul, so why am I still nervous?* Maldeor moaned in his sleep and threw off the sheets. The silk felt sticky and suffocating. By his cushioned hollow, his leather armor was laid out piece by piece, with his sword alongside it.

Outside, the sun, deep yellow like Yin Soul's eyes, rose slowly above the horizon.

You will come back tomorrow! YOU WILL!

A strange wind picked up in the valley. Vitelline, brown, and khaki, the archaeopteryx empire's tooth-edged flag fluttered wildly above the castle. The design in the center, an archaeopteryx wing, shook like a drowning bird's limb. Then the wind drifted lower and lifted the curtains of Maldeor's chamber.

One bright ray of sun seized the chance and darted through.

It fell across the face of the sleeping Maldeor, shining on the teeth of his half-opened beak. *Will I go back? Will I need Yin Soul's help?* The curtains fell back again and the light was gone, but Maldeor started to shiver and his breathing grew faster and faster. *No, I don't . . . I don't! I am myself, and only myself. Is that you, raven messenger? Fly back—I will not go! I shall not see Yin Soul today! Be gone, Yin Soul. Away! Away! Away! When I get the hero's sword, I won't need your potion anymore.* His claws fluttered aimlessly on his embroidered silk sheets like heavy moths; suddenly they scrunched up the fabric.

Maldeor sat bolt upright, his eyes bulging like eggs, his claws gripping his wide-open beak.

"Ah—ah—ah . . . !"

The unearthly scream tore through the castle, ripping apart the silence. In frightened unison, the three hundred birds of the archaeopteryx army sat up rigid on their perches.

Maldeor had a toothache.

He rolled to the left: The pain erupted there. He rolled to the right, and it did not falter. Whimpering, screaming, cursing, he slapped his own cheeks left and right, pulled feathers out of his face, and even flipped onto his back, feet peddling in the air. "It is Yin Soul's doing!" he gasped to himself finally as he performed a headstand propped against his castle wall and found temporary relief.

"Servants, call the royal dentist!"

When the bird came, Maldeor gestured to the tooth that pained him and ordered it to be pulled.

"No, Your Majesty. It is seriously infected!" the dentist said, recoiling. "The only way is to take medicine, but it is highly unpredictable—"

"Nonsense. Bring it here!"

After swallowing a teaspoonful, Maldeor leaped out of his chamber to check the progress of the sky carriage he had ordered to be built.

In his courtyard, a wild-looking structure was being assembled by sawdust-covered carpenters. It was shaped like a kite, with tough canvas stretched over a bamboo frame. There was a hollow in the very center, where

Maldeor would ride.

"Your Majesty, we've gotten a dozen sturdy goose slaves to pull your carriage."

"Harness them immediately! We go tonight!" *I will outsmart you, Yin Soul!* Maldeor thought as he drank more of the medicine. *I shall be the hero!*

Many harmful things in life are seductively beautiful,
like poisonous mushrooms.
—FROM THE *OLD SCRIPTURE*

13
TREASURE CAVE

Robins hovered above a huge tapestry laid flat on the ground. The design of yin and yang looked like two huge white and black tadpoles swimming together, encircled by orderly lines. It was a surprising sight.

"I knew you would come," the old robin said evenly as he held the sparkling red Leasorn. "Some say I have the gift of foresight. When I go up the White Cap Mountains and perch in the mysterious fog, I see snippets of present, past, future . . . and these, along with the yin and yang, reveal things to me." He shook a clawful of polished maple wood sticks. "I saw the two of you flying over the ocean, which is why we came to meet you today. We cannot thank you enough. Your places are in the mountains and woods, yet you risked your life to make the treacherous journey across the water to return this to us. This devotion, this virtue, sadly, is rare now. If you are not heroes, who else can be?"

"Sir." Fleydur bowed. "We are only following the ways of our hearts: The true ways of a bird."

"If you can see sparks of the future . . ." Ewingerale began but faltered when he realized everybird was listening. Then he said boldly, "I was wondering if . . . you happened to see a myna, stout, with a staff and a wooden berry strung around his neck . . . Or maybe"— Ewingerale exchanged looks with the eagle—"a white dovelike bird?"

Everybird quieted as the robin flung his sticks onto the tapestry below. He flew around and around the yin and yang, his maple-leaf headdress rustling, for what seemed like an eternity. "Go south," he whispered as he orbited, seemingly not at all conscious of the woodpecker's question. "Go south, where icebergs float, where ice storms whirl. You are needed there, before Hero's Day, when the hero will claim the sword. Danger is coming. There will be slashing teeth and fluttering wings over the ocean. Look for a special current in the sea. The air above it will carry you. Quickly, before it is too late."

As afternoon came on, Wind-voice and Stormac, after flying all day, finally passed over the southernmost tip of the land, Cape Beak, and flew toward the sea. An archipelago of tiny cays and coral reefs dotted the waters below. It seemed to the two travelers that somebird had scattered stars on the water.

"You want to prevent Maldeor from getting the hero's sword, but tell me, how many birds out there are like him, evil and wanting to become a hero?" Stormac said suddenly as the vastness of the ocean sent a foreboding chill down him. "How can you prevent them all?"

"I want to do what I can. It's better than watching those cruel birds and doing nothing. If we lead the way, others might stop other wrongdoers." Above them, huge clouds that looked like fluffy white versions of the Skythunder Mountains were suspended in the air. Windvoice gazed at them dreamily. "Then someday the whole world will be peaceful."

"But it's a hard, hard thing," Stormac grumbled.

"Becoming a hero myself is easier than flapping around hampering the bad birds."

"I hope that you will become a hero someday," Wind-voice said.

The clouds turned dark gray. Eyeing them warily, the two exhausted birds looked around for a place to rest. Suddenly a cloud shifted in the distance, and in the open stretch of sky they saw a spectacular mansion of exotic trees right by a clear fountain.

"Wow! The birds there must be so rich!" Stormac yelled. He rowed his wings with renewed vigor, adjusting his direction so that he headed straight for the mansion. "I can't wait to get there!"

"It seems like a mirage, Stormac," Wind-voice said doubtfully. Sure enough, as they neared the mansion it disappeared. The two flew more slowly now, feeling more tired than ever. Now the sky was turning dark pea green.

Wind-voice caught sight of a young gull in the distance. He called to him, "Where can we find an island big enough for us weary travelers to rest?"

The young bird flew up to greet them. "My tribe lives on an island not far away." He had a harpoon in his claws.

The two birds gladly followed the gull, but the mighty

wind was treacherous. Whenever they tried to double their speed, it blew more savagely, enough to make them feel as if they were not making progress, or even slipping backward. The sea below churned and churned. They could hear the waves crashing and the foam hissing. What was frightening, however, was that they could see none of it, as the rain clouds above deposited what seemed like an ocean's worth of water upon them.

"It's storm season," explained the gull over the wails and howls of the wind. "Do be careful!"

"I don't think we can fly against this wind for much longer," Stormac cried.

"There!" Wind-voice yelled, spotting something on one of the islands. "It looks like a cave!"

"You're right!"

The gull squinted at the blurry dark shape and called to them, "I've seen it from a distance before, but I've never been inside. Still, anywhere is better than being out in the weather now!"

"Quick!" Stormac called. They landed just inside the cave, exhausted and wet. The air was damp and warm, but there was a faint smell of metal and drying seaweed. They all edged backward out of the wind.

Of the three, Stormac disliked water the most. He backed into the cave as fast as possible, but suddenly he stopped. A sharp, painful prick on his spine sent shivers through him. Was that the knife of an enemy who had slyly waited for this chance to kill them all when they were vulnerable? He stiffened. His blood went cold, colder than the freezing seawater.

With his heart throbbing, he jerked out his staff and whirled around.

"Stop where you are!" he shouted at the darkness.

There was a faint hiss as Wind-voice lit a match. The quivering circle of light fell upon the enemy.

With a gasp, Stormac dropped his staff and stumbled, sitting down hard. The other birds stared.

The enemy was a grinning gold statue of a merry little bird holding silver flowers, gemstones embedded in the center of each blossom. Its "sword" was only a long, protruding leaf in the metal bouquet.

They looked at one another and found themselves all tensed as if ready to fight. Stormac started to laugh.

"Just a statue!" he tittered, rubbing the sore spot on his back. "Oh my! Getting all upset over this little dancing bird with the flowers."

But the gull said, "Look!" and Wind-voice lit a second match.

Beyond the statue, in big piles, were coins and bars of gold and silver; strings of pearls; necklaces of rubies, emeralds, and sapphires; rings of diamonds, opals, and amber; bracelets of jade, turquoise, and crystal. They sparkled with a dangerous glimmer in the match's light.

They all noticed a deep blue stone, faceted and faintly glowing, a little ways off. Wind-voice hopped over and picked the gem up. He turned it over, finding markings.

"What! It's the sacred gemstone that was stolen from my tribesbirds and friends!" From behind Wind-voice, the gull's voice grew shrill. "I'm flabbergasted!"

They peered at it silently. *Another gem with a clue,* thought Wind-voice. He tried to read it, but his matches were spent and the light was too dim.

"The pieces of the stand for the gemstone are here, too!" The seagull collected scattered pieces of coral and started reassembling them. Wind-voice and Stormac roused themselves and helped as well. As Wind-voice wandered over near one wall, Stormac and the gull looked near the other. Suddenly a great sparkle caught the myna's eye. It was a piece of carved red crystal, and it was shaped like a strawberry. Stormac lifted the crystal strawberry up and compared it side by side with the wooden strawberry around his neck. His eyes grew wider when he saw how similar they were. Surely a crystal pendant was better to wear than a flimsy wooden one. "Is this your tribe's?" he asked the gull, who shook his head.

"We'll go to your tribe and return the gem tomorrow, after the weather breaks," Wind-voice was saying.

The gull nodded. The gem's stand was assembled now and held the gem. "But Great Spirit!" he whispered, and shivered. He shuffled his webbed feet, edging toward the cave's entrance, away from the horde of valuables. "To think that we are to spend the night with this."

Stormac's big eyes reflected the glow of the treasure, and he murmured, "But that's silver! That's gold! Look, all sorts of trinkets! What riches! They would last lifetimes." He also thought again of the crystal strawberry.

"Riches that have an evil glow," Wind-voice said.

"Pirates' loot," agreed the gull.

"Don't touch them, Stormac," Wind-voice warned. "If we take anything that belongs to birds we don't know, we might be mistaken for the actual robbers if we chance to meet those birds!"

"Oh." Stormac moaned slightly but joined the others in moving away from the loot. He wanted the crystal strawberry.

That night, as the gale still raged, the three birds stayed put. While the two other birds slept, Stormac's eyes were open, riveted on the treasures, feasting on the radiance. *I could leave my staff in this cave tomorrow morning and pretend to forget it,* he thought. *Then I'll be able to come back to retrieve it* . . . After he managed to fall asleep, he dreamed of the little statue of the bird holding the flowers dancing around and around, chanting in a singsong voice to the clinking of jewels and coins, "Oh, look at us! Gold! Silver! Take us, take us, take us and you will be happy forever . . ."

The next morning the sky was so clear that it seemed as if it had been washed and scrubbed clean of yesterday's dirty gray clouds.

Stormac was quieter than usual all morning. The three birds had a soggy meal and left the pirates' cave, flying toward the gull's island home, the biggest island in the archipelago.

Since Wind-voice was preoccupied with the discovery of the seagull's gem, Stormac managed to avoid his attention, flying behind his two companions. By and by he said to the young seabird, "Ah! Forgot my staff. I've got to fetch it. Be back in a couple of wing beats' time. Don't tell Wind-voice. I don't want him to worry."

The island appeared on the horizon. The seagull, sensing nothing wrong in particular, nodded and kept silent. The myna sped away.

Stormac's wing beats grew quicker the closer he got to the cave. When he reached it, he snatched up his staff, lying under the flower-bearing statue, and hopped farther inside. Within a few seconds he was standing, lost in ecstasy, the prized crystal strawberry in his claws. How realistic it was! His beak almost watered. He was about to untie his necklace and replace the drab pendant with the new one when a thought struck him—if he went back with the crystal berry on his neck, Wind-voice was bound to notice and question him. If he stuffed it somewhere in a knapsack, Wind-voice might see it sooner or later, too.

The conversation with Wind-voice from the day before floated into his mind. A voice deep inside him said, *You know it is wrong, Stormac. What about your wooden strawberry? Remember what it is supposed to remind you of—your past.*

"I have no need for this," Stormac said firmly. He

flung the strawberry away with all his might. He must not be lured. The crystal landed somewhere deeper in the cave.

He was about to turn and leave when he saw a beautiful ivory club, its handle studded with tiny rubies, laying within a few clawsteps. In an instant a picture formed in his mind—Stormac the myna, in battle against the archaeopteryxes, wielding his glittering white club, famed in legend and song. He dropped his shabby wooden staff, ran over, picked the club up, and hefted it. It wasn't like the crystal strawberry, after all. This was a *weapon*. It was useful.

But then the little voice inside him said, *Your wooden staff is good enough for you. It's tough, realiable, and solid, like you are. You know that you just want this elaborate thing; you don't* need *it.*

Stormac reluctantly let the sparkling weapon fall from his claws. "That's true. Must get the needs and wants straightened out," he muttered.

His eyes, searching for his old wooden staff on the floor, focused next on a compass. Wind-voice hadn't seen that yesterday. Now, this was definitely something necessary. It would be foolish, after all, to travel so far with nothing to guide them. They might be grateful for it later on. The voice inside him hummed in agreement.

He picked the instrument up with confidence and would have marched out of the cave if he hadn't suddenly smelled a terrible odor, then felt a shadow fall across him.

"Shiver my feathers! If that isn't one of those birdies on the archaeopteryxes' wanted posters," a harsh voice exclaimed.

This time the enemy was real.

*Self-blame stings more
than putting salt on one's wounds.*
—FROM THE OLD SCRIPTURE

14
BROTHER FOREVER

W here's Stormac?" Wind-voice said quizzically when he and the gull almost arrived at the island.

"Oh, he forgot his staff and he went back to fetch it. He said not to worry; he would be back quickly. I think he will have no problem finding us here."

Indeed, the large island was easy to locate and the place where the seabirds lived was hard to miss. Dozens of nesting petrels, gulls, albatrosses, and tropic birds had formed an alliance, called the Qua.

Chief Aqual's sallow cheeks lifted into a smile when he saw the gem. "Thank you, thank you! Those cruel pirates have limited us in many ways . . . but now our treasure is back. This calls for a celebration. Take out the stores from our cellar and share our food with our new friend!"

All the birds present hushed as a dozen fishes were carried out to the stone table.

"Please help yourself to our fish," Aqual said kindly, but Wind-voice was rooted to the stone ledge. The fishes were curled up as if in embarrassment of their half-rotten, mildewed state. One fish's round shriveled eye stared at Wind-voice. *How poor these birds must be, and still they share their food!* he thought. When Wind-voice looked up, he found that dozens of birds had crowded around the table.

"Why don't you eat too?" he asked.

"Guests first," said the leader, smiling.

Wind-voice ate a pungent sliver out of politeness. Soon, the rest of the seabirds joined in, rapidly devouring the fishes. A sealed pot was carried up to them by several tottering gulls. It was the second course. The gulls opened the clay jar, and a slippery, shiny green-gray mass, cut in thin slices, was solemnly hooked out and placed in scallop shells. Beaks opened and murmurings of *aah* swept through the crowd. Some birds drooled in anticipation. Right beside Wind-voice, a small gull chick's mouth gaped open and it nearly fainted at the sight of the rare food.

"Spicy pickled kelp," said Aqual with evident delight.

For the final course, the gulls served coconuts. Most of the fruits were not green but a deep brown, and the few green ones were unripe. The sour odor that came from the bruised skin of one was sickening.

The chief had been beaming at Wind-voice, but now he looked ashamed. "Alas," he said apologetically, "the coconut trees on our islands have just been raided by the pirates. However, do try them; they are more nutritious than the preserves, and being so aged, they have actually acquired a flavor very close to ale."

"I have something to contribute to the feast as well." Wind-voice took off his sack and poured half of his remaining supplies into a pile. The gulls stared at the acorn-flour cakes, raisins, thistleseed bread, and dried worms before them. Wind-voice took a fragment of acorn and ate it to demonstrate. Small seabirds unknowingly drifted forward, their beaks opening and closing in time with his. The chicks leaned out of their nests, their heads bobbing with hunger.

"Thank you, thank you!" Aqual said thickly, and the group of seabirds fell upon the food, eating happily, saving bits for the old, the young, and the weak among them.

Contented, thankful smiles grew on faces as the food diminished. Wind-voice told them of his journey to stop Maldeor from getting the hero's sword.

"I have heard that the carvings on the gem contain some hidden wisdom," said Aqual thoughtfully. "Still, we have nobird with us who can read Avish, I'm afraid. Our lives are so hard now that all must strive to find food every day; we have no time for scholarship." He held out the gemstone and gazed at it sadly.

Wind-voice leaned in. "It looks like it says, 'Find flowers amid ice.' Avish! Oh, I miss Ewingerale," said Wind-voice slowly, then looked up in alarm. "And where's Stormac? He should be here by now."

"Look here, mateys! What a nice catch we've got!" a pirate sniggered, scratching a salt-crusted beak.

The twenty or so jaegers, skuas, and frigate birds chortled. Sleek and shimmering in scraps of silk and satin, they piled around the entrance of the cave. Stormac looked around frantically. He was trapped.

Captain Rag-foot squeezed himself in front, waving a curved dagger. "Stop the fool laughing, you lot." A skua, speckled brown and riddled with fleas, he wore strings of shark teeth draped around his neck and shoulders, and the webbing on one of his feet was mangled.

Rag-foot jabbed his dagger at the myna. "My scout here says you were spotted with the white one, the one worth the biggest reward. Where has he gone?"

"You must have seen a small cloud." Stormac tried to muster his bravery. "I don't know who you're speaking of."

"Cloud! Imprudent bird, tell us what you know." The pirates stepped closer.

"There's nothing to tell."

Rag-foot clacked his beak. "Certainly there are things to tell! Why are you here? This is our cave."

"I was—"

"Passing by? A woodland myna, yes, very likely. Your companion took the blue gemstone, too." Rag-foot stared at the myna for a long time. Stormac could not think of anything to say. Around him, pirates twiddled with their bludgeons and knives.

The silence was abruptly broken by smacking eating sounds. "Hmm . . . the reward for this one is plenty, but it says only the head is required," Rag-foot called to another pirate, a smirk settling on his face. "He looks nice and juicy. Lots of fat on him. Seize him and build a cooking fire."

To Stormac's dismay, he was bound to his own staff. "You careless fool," he moaned to himself, but it was too late for regrets now.

A pirate pulled out an enormous cooking pan the size of a tub. Two birds crouched on their bellies to blow at the coals, and a third poured coconut oil into the pan.

"Now," said Captain Rag-foot, "pluck him!"

Beaks shot forward and grabbed Stormac's feathers. His head spun and he writhed in pain. "No! Stop!" he cried.

Rag-foot gestured and his minions stepped back. "Tell us immediately where the white bird went," he growled. "Speak up!"

"I don't know," Stormac whimpered. A pirate came forward and tore another clump of feathers away. "I don't know . . . I really . . . don't . . ."

The captain shook his strings of shark teeth and glared. "Enough! Fry him!"

A dirty seabird wearing a bandanna dragged Stormac and his staff to the sizzling pan. Four birds, two on each side, raised him over the pan and lowered him slowly.

Stormac screamed and screamed as the hot oil

splattered onto his bare skin where his feathers had been torn away. "If you lead us to the white bird, you might not end up in our bellies," Captain Rag-foot added sweetly as he squashed a flea in his feathers.

No, Stormac thought. *I can't. Not Wind-voice. I can't betray him.* But the pain filled his mind until he could think of nothing else. "All right! I will!" he agreed.

The pirates pulled him from the pan. One came forward and snapped a chain around Stormac's right foot. Three pirates held the other end of the leash.

"You must promise to draw him out in the open for us. Don't you dare try leading us on some false trail," the pirate captain warned. "Or there will be worse to come for you . . ."

Stormac gulped, nodding.

All along the way, he flew as slowly as he dared. His eyes couldn't see properly, but this time the mirage was not in the sky but in his head. He remembered how, when others, even Fisher, had sometimes had faint doubts about him because of his past, Wind-voice had never seemed to doubt him for an instant. He remembered the times when he had fought side by side with Wind-voice, together driving the enemy away. He remembered how Wind-voice proclaimed that they were brothers. What a wonderful friend Wind-voice was! The bird was always caring for others.

Now I am betraying him, Stormac thought. So selfish. So terrible. The tears of shame in his eyes nearly blinded him. Could he truly do it?

"Where is Stormac?" Wind-voice said again, pacing the cliffs in agitation. He looked up and scanned the sky . . . and this time he saw a figure winging his way. It was the myna, all right, yet strangely he was not holding his staff. A chain trailed from his feet.

Wind-voice jumped into the air to greet his friend.

Stormac banked, screaming, "Stop, Wind-voice! Go back! Pirates!"

The myna darted toward Wind-voice, wings outstretched as a hissing rain of arrows filled the sky behind him. But none hit Wind-voice. The myna's outspread wings protected the white bird from harm.

Wind-voice dove forward, but before he could reach Stormac, a swarm of figures surged up and over the myna, blocking him from sight. In the motley group of outcasts a bedraggled frigate bird held an outrageously curved sword while a swaggering jaeger clutched a spiked bludgeon. Wind-voice saw flashes of silk and gold among the extravagant weaponry. Despite their diversity, what unified them was their greed and their stink of rotten fish.

"Stormac!" Wind-voice screamed. He charged, spinning his sword to hack the pirates away. Behind him, the seagulls burst out of their caves, holding fish spears and swinging rocks on ropes.

"Robbers!" they screeched.

"Murderers!"

"We won't stand this anymore!"

The battle began.

Each of the pirates realized he could take advantage of the new opportunities arising from the melee. "Look! Tender young birds," one frigate bird yelled as he pointed at a row of nests on a ledge. He landed below the ledge before the parents could stop him. Fluffy fulmar chicks peeped over the edge with open mouths, and arc after arc of foul-smelling vomit hit the pirate in the face. "Ahh!" The frigate bird staggered back, wiping at his sticky face.

"Silly of you. Fulmar chicks always do that!" another pirate snapped at him. "Let's go over *there*! There is the gemstone that we need to steal back." However, Aqual and four terns pelted him with broken oyster shells before he could get near the gem.

Though the Qua, the seabird alliance, had only crude

weaponry, they numbered no less than a hundred. Crowded onto the guano-streaked ledges, ten birds fought with every pirate.

A tern dressed in checkered pink and red silk swiped at Wind-voice, who ducked and sliced off a piece of the fabric, trying to fight his way toward Stormac's fallen body.

Finally Rag-foot tried to organize his dirty pirates. "Now, all of you, get that strange dove! Get him! He's worth a bag of treasures!" he shouted. The seabirds swarmed protectively around Wind-voice, swinging the rocks on their ropes. Then a well-aimed rock slammed on Rag-foot's ragged toes. He screeched in pain and plummeted toward the sea. The other pirates stopped what they were doing and followed their captain, trying to steal the bangles and shark-teeth ornaments from their own leader. They fought among themselves. A few more blows from the Qua and they were driven away, still quarreling and wondering why they had come in the first place.

After the skirmish, Wind-voice dashed down the cliff to where Stormac had fallen. The myna was lying unmoving on the beach. Every time the tide surged up, he bobbed and was carried a few inches farther toward the ocean. The sand around him was wet with blood.

In a few more moments, Stormac would be lost in the tide. Wind-voice hovered above him, gripping Stormac's clenched claws. Another wave hit them. Wind-voice could feel the pull of the receding tide as it swirled around Stormac's body. *I must be quick. . . .* Wind-voice ground his beak through his tears. *You won't take him, ocean . . . he is my friend.* He flapped his wings harder, dug at the sand with his free claw.

Then he felt Stormac's balled claws uncurl. "Let go, Wind-voice. It's all right." Another wave battered against them, and Wind-voice felt their grip loosen. He saw something faint—a sad smile?—on the myna's face. "I won't hinder you anymore," Stormac whispered.

No! Wind-voice lunged at his friend, and an overwhelming strength he did not know he had possessed coursed through his blood. Suddenly he and Stormac were the only two birds in the world, and all he cared about was saving the myna. He held on fast to his dear friend, turned back toward the shore, and advanced, one strenuous wing beat at a time. The sun hanging low at the edge of the cliff seemed to burn into him.

At last, the sand held firm under their claws. With one wing supporting Stormac, Wind-voice struggled toward the cliff. The myna's warm blood flowed onto his feathers.

Stormac coughed, his whole body shaking. He could feel Wind-voice's strong heartbeat as he limped along.

"A few more steps now," Wind-voice said. The seabirds gathered around them, staring. Aqual started forward as if to help, but Wind-voice wanted to support Stormac alone.

On a sunny patch of sand Stormac crumpled softly.

"The wounds on your back!" Wind-voice said, trying to pull out the arrows. His voice was barely audible.

"Right now, the pain in my heart is far worse than that of my skin." Stormac struggled to lift his eyes and look at Wind-voice. "It's too late to regret, I know. It's strange, isn't it . . . when I finally realize I'm wrong, I'm miles astray. When I am eager to seize life, its end is here." With a feeble cough, the warrior turned his head back and pecked at the knot on his necklace. "Life's a battle . . . I've lost. . . ."

"No . . . you've won, brilliantly," Wind-voice whispered. He looked down in shock as Stormac held out the shining red berry necklace to him. "Stormac . . ."

"Take it, take it, please. Then I will always be with you . . ." Stormac paused and shuddered. "All my life I keep making the same mistakes. Falling for the same temptations. Most of the time I knew beforehand that something was wrong . . . but I still did it. I . . . I will never know tomorrow."

Wind-voice crouched lower at the myna's side, trying not to cry. The berry charm was heavy. It seemed to carry all the weight of the world. "You'll be fine. Tomorrow will be better, brother."

"Do you still regard me as your brother?"

"Yes, always, always."

"Brother . . . tomorrow . . ." Stormac's eyes suddenly grew fixed on the setting sun. His beak opened rapidly twice, in two shallow breaths, and then he was still.

The seagulls dug a hole in the rocky turf big enough for Stormac's body. They stood in a row, white mourning sashes fluttering, as the myna was lowered into his grave. In the background, the wail of a traditional funeral tune sounded from a giant conch shell.

Wind-voice wished Winger were there to play his harp, or Fleydur were there to sing. Tears rolled down his cheeks. *My brother forever*, he thought. Wind-voice felt utterly alone and chilled in the seawind.

When we suffer the worst hardships,
our destination may be just a step away.
—FROM THE OLD SCRIPTURE

15

THE BATTLE
OF THE ICE PALACE

"Y our Majesty," said Kawaka, thumping his claws on his chest, "the ocean is in view."

Maldeor gulped down a cup of the medicine for his toothache. He knew, despite the pain distracting him, that it was time to organize his notes. During the journey from Castlewood, he had written feverishly whenever they set up camp. All his observations, his thoughts, even his conversations with Yin Soul he scribbled down.

He took out a carefully wrapped package, undid all the layers of linen, and smoothed each page of the stack of papers and notes inside. His eyes trailed over the words of wisdom Yin Soul had imparted to him. "His words are deep and true. Maybe it would have been better if I had listened to him. . . ." Maldeor whispered to himself. He shook his head, dismissing his doubts. He cut a piece of leather, wrapped it around the paper, and bit holes along the spine. After binding the pages securely with leather thongs, he caught up his quill, dipped it in gold ink, and scrawled on the cover:

BOOK OF HERESY

He paced up and down in his tent, waiting for the ink to dry. His sword, sheathed by his side, clanked as he restlessly moved about.

Thoughtfully he drew the sword and gazed fondly at the plain steel blade.

"You and I," he cried in a theatrical voice, "we have been faithful companions. But soon, I shall have another weapon. You have served me well."

His eyes lit up as an idea popped into his head.

He spun around and scuttled to the other side of the tent, where a mirror was propped. Head swaying, drunk with moonlight and arrogance, he raised his sword high in the air and waved it.

"Hero, hero," he proclaimed to the mirror, admiring the effect.

Then he sheathed the sword once more, picked up the *Book of Heresy*, wrapped a layer of oilcloth around it, and flew off alone into the night. He would find a place to hide his book for safekeeping. He knew that if by any chance things went wrong on Kauria, his thoughts and ideas would survive him.

The island of the seagulls faded into the distance behind Wind-voice as he soared over the waves. All the clues he had gathered so far made no sense to him. *Find flowers amid ice.* But no plants thrived when winter sent snow and ice to cover the land.

"Well, south to the glaciers is as good a guess as any,"

he said to himself. Had he been mad to go on this quest, just as Stormac had told him? Had he been too unrealistic to think that he, a former slave, a fledgling with no living family and no tribe, could do anything to help the hero?

Stormac, maybe you were right, he thought as he flew. *Maybe finding the gems is a wild errand. I'm sorry, so sorry, that I brought you with me. You'd still be alive if I hadn't . . .*

Blinded by tears, he didn't notice the low, dark clouds swirling up over the horizon until suddenly he was engulfed in them. The wind that had been carrying him steadily along was suddenly uneven. Gusts blew up under his wings and tossed him from side to side.

The clouds ahead of Wind-voice seemed to take on a shape. He stared in astonishment as a bird made of black mist spread ghostly wings and raised its head, lifting a huge beak. For a moment, before the winds tore the figure apart, it had looked like the toucan, rising once more to break his chains.

Everything had seemed hopeless at that moment, too, when he'd been tied to that log in the river. Yet, somehow, he had survived. It would be foolish to give up now. He would keep trying.

I was named for the wind, Wind-voice thought. *I'll let*

the wind decide what to do. He stiffened his wings, letting the wind take him where it would. The storm tossed and buffeted him but carried him gradually southwest.

"Look at that, Fleydur!" Ewingerale cried. The two birds had been riding southward on the cold sea wind for two days now. "A huge white iceberg!

"The old robin prophet predicted that there would be slashing teeth and fluttering wings in the southern ocean. Did he mean that archaeopteryxes would come?"

Winger did a quick calculation. "Today is Hero's Day. The archaeopteryx emperor is looking for the sword. Why would he be so frantic to come here? Unless he is scouring the four corners of the world, trying to find the strange gemstones fallen from the sky?"

When they reached the glacier, they found a penguin standing on the slope, about to jump into the ocean.

"We have urgent news for your tribe," Fleydur cried. "Something terrible may happen."

"The archaeopteryxes, yes," Ewingerale said. "They are finally coming south."

"Archaeopteryxes! Here!" The penguin gasped. He immediately led them inside a smooth, blue-white tunnel. Ice sculptures glistened at them from both sides.

They traveled through the sparkling corridors. Many penguins slid by, sometimes in adjoining tunnels, their black-and-white reflections contorted into mysterious shapes by the undulating ice walls. At last they were led to a huge penguin sitting on an ice ledge in a pale blue hall. She was introduced as Lady Gwendeleine, and Ewingerale told her the travails of their journey.

When he mentioned the gemstone, Lady Gwendeleine interrupted him.

"Gemstone—sky! How . . . I mean, how do you know about it?" Lady Gwendeleine was surprised.

"My own family had a strange faceted purple stone with carvings on it," Fleydur confided to her. "We knew from the start it was something special—it just appeared out of nowhere. I thought we were the only ones to have something like that. Our journeys over the last few months showed that a couple of other tribes spread out over the archaeopteryx territories have similar gems, only differently colored."

"They've something to do with the legend of the hero, and the hero's sword!" Ewingerale said. "The sword is in Kauria, Island of Paradise. Today is Hero's Day. If I'm guessing right, Maldeor will certainly be among the archaeopteryxes who shall head here."

One penguin adviser wearing ice glasses spoke up. "Perhaps the archaeopteryxes are heading for an island a bit north of us," he informed the eagle and the woodpecker. "It is a strange land hidden in the mists, which seems to move with the tide. Some time ago, when we swam to its shores, we were greeted by bright purple and green birds and given fruits to eat."

"Yes, there is that island. Perhaps it is Kauria," Lady Gwendeleine reflected. "But they might be coming for something else, too, because we *do* have a gemstone. It's pale blue." She touched a panel of ice near her throne. The panel swung open to reveal a secret compartment. She took out a beautiful gemstone that seemed almost like a polished piece of ice.

"'Find the bird who flies through waters,'" Winger read. "Kauria sounds more magical by the minute. If it's so difficult to find, the archaeopteryxes might mistake your island for Kauria. If they do, then we can take advantage of it. Certainly none of us wants the archaeopteryx emperor to get the sword. If we keep delaying Maldeor till Hero's Day is over, then he won't be able to stop the true hero from getting the sword."

"You're right. We will distract them so that they will lose track of time. We will create a diversion with feast and song," Lady Gwendeleine said.

Ewingerale's eyes twinkled as he whispered more ideas to the penguins, who nodded in agreement.

"My lady!" A small penguin suddenly slid into view from a tunnel hidden in the ice and got up to salute. An ice telescope was hung around his neck. "We have sighted them, coming in a straight course!"

The advancing archaeopteryx army, in full glory, swept across the sky in one huge V. Maldeor made sure the tip of this deadly avian arrowhead pointed southwest. He was headed toward Kauria. Perched on his great kite, Maldeor was protected inside the V. He frowned at a dark gray mass in the western sky. The air current became bumpier and bumpier.

Then, all of a sudden, a huge white streak split the sky ahead. A terrible wind rippled the archaeopteryx ranks. Maldeor's carriage bucked like a living thing. Gripping the bamboo frame tightly with his claws, his cloak flapping madly like extra wings, he screeched, "Careful! Careful! Veer a little east and avoid the storm!" Thunder rumbled. Raindrops the size of grapes pelted them.

Maldeor uncurled a whip and snapped it above the bodies of the twelve geese pulling his carriage. "Faster, faster! If we get too wet, we'll fall down!" A goose on the left could not keep up with the rest and was dropping altitude from fatigue. Growling, Maldeor leaned forward and cut off the leather harness from the faltering slave. The goose plummeted down and disappeared in a white circle of foam.

Without the drag, Maldeor's carriage moved faster. He waved his dripping wings in the air. "Don't let the lightning strike us!"

It's never wise to battle with the army of nature. The archaeopteryxes drifted about like a tattered group of beggars. Once the storm had passed, they continued on south, faster than ever, trying to make up for lost time. They did not realize that they had missed Kauria altogether. While his feathers dried, Maldeor peered through a telescope. "Look, there's Kauria!" he cried to Kawaka, his toothache temporarily forgotten as his confidence returned. He pointed to a huge white iceberg. "Direct the army to it!"

"The clue said, 'Find flowers amid ice.' There's ice on the island, but no flowers anywhere!" a scholar flying nearby protested.

"Fool! Can't you see that the clue is a literary metaphor? That huge iceberg looks just like a white water lily. Of *course* this is Kauria. Onward!" he yelled triumphantly.

When the archaeopteryx army arrived above the island, Maldeor ordered guards to span overhead so that any other bird coming to find the sword would be stopped and killed. He, the geese, and the rest of his army landed. They folded up the carriage.

"Welcome to our island," a penguin said, greeting him. "Come in!"

Maldeor followed him, gaping at the intricacy he saw all around him. Though he was familiar with riches and luxury, the mysterious splendor here was a sight to see. Some walls were so thin they were like glass, while others let only a blue shimmering light filter through.

"This is indeed like paradise!" he exclaimed as he slid along the corridors. He grinned with delight when the penguin bowed and gestured for them to come into a low, wide hall. "What hospitality! A feast!"

Scallops and clams were arranged in circles around heaps of pinkish krill. There was shining black fish roe

and diced mackerel, shrimp, and seaweed. A huge silvery fish, the catch of the day, lay on a platter. Two penguins on either side were busy at work, using an ice saw to slice off succulent steaks. The centerpiece, a speckled red starfish, was the most eye-catching of all.

Most of the archaeopteryxes dug in eagerly, but Maldeor ate little because he kept thinking of the sword. "Thank you for all this," he said politely to Lady

Gwendeleine. "I was wondering, perhaps, if you might show me the hero's sword?"

"Which one do you mean? We have many. But a long way you've come! After you've eaten and rested, we'll show you around."

Maldeor did not argue. He knew that he and his soldiers were in bad shape after their exhausting journey. He held an ice shard against his cheek to ease the pain of his toothache. All through the feast, while his soldiers buried their faces in their plates, he stole glances at the corners and the tunnels. *Where is the phoenix, Pepheroh? Where are the other toucans?* Then he caught sight of Ewingerale and Fleydur. *What! Why are a woodpecker and an eagle here? Are they also trying to find the sword? The eagle looks tough.*

Maldeor signaled to one of his knights to keep an eye on the two. *But then . . . maybe they actually* do *live on this cold island. It's magical. Perhaps the phoenix and the rest are hidden somewhere. Perhaps this is a test.*

After the feast, the penguins gave a concert on their ice xylophones. Maldeor continued to worry. Today was Hero's Day. The atmosphere was pleasant enough, but the weather was too cold for an archaeopteryx. If he could get the sword immediately, he would fly back to warmer lands.

When the last music piece ended, Maldeor strode fretfully up to Lady Gwendeleine. "Lady, would you be so kind as to show me your swords now?"

With Winger at her side, Gwendeleine nodded. "Come and bring the special swords," she called into the empty tunnels, as planned. There was a soft pattering of feet on ice as stocky penguins entered, balancing weaponry on cushions on their toes. Each bowed courteously and asked Maldeor, "Sir, is this it?"

Besides steel and iron swords, there were even ones made of ice. After inspecting twenty of them, he started to feel foolish and angry. Yin Soul had hinted that the magical sword had the eighth gemstone on its hilt. None of the swords here had a gemstone anywhere. *There's something behind this,* he thought, narrowing his eyes. Something wasn't right. Again his doubts clouded his mind, and then quickly he formed a plan.

He turned around and smiled pleasantly at a penguin scholar. "It seems you have guests here? There's a woodpecker and an eagle."

"Yes, sometimes birds come and go. Seabirds are the majority," said the penguin scholar.

"I can see why. It's so beautiful here. Even the toucans would want to come."

The penguin scholar beamed. "I sure hope they

would! They're neighbors, after all."

Too late, the penguin realized his mistake.

The feathers on Maldeor's face all rose on end, and his eyes squeezed into ugly slits. *First my shriveling wing, then my toothache, now this!* he thought. "You tricked me! You're trying to delay me further!" He seized the penguin scholar by the scruff of his neck, holding the end of his sword against the penguin's forehead. "You know where it really is. Tell me, which direction?"

"It's not . . . I . . ."

"Tell me!" Maldeor bellowed. The sword point shook. Blood seeped out of a cut between the penguin's eyes.

"How dare you!" Lady Gwendeleine raised a flipper-like wing. "Release the scholar. Stop!"

Maldeor seized the scholar even tighter and ordered his soldiers to charge the penguins.

Only now did he realize how low the ceiling was. He could not fly. His troops charged as best as they could, staggering and slipping on the ice, but Maldeor could tell they were too full to be in good shape for battle.

The penguins grabbed the heavy ice plates. They hurled them like discuses into the ranks of the charging knights, then turned around and ran into the tunnels.

"Kill them! Kill them!" Maldeor commanded. His

soldiers blundered together in a heavy mass as they chased after the penguins in the tunnels. The ice floor collapsed beneath their weight. Screaming, they disappeared as the black ocean closed over their heads.

When the remaining soggy troops finally drove the penguins into the wide hall of the throne room, penguins kept popping in and out of the tunnels, agile and quick. They ducked blows so that the swords of the archaeopteryxes hacked onto the ice pillars instead.

"Be careful! No!" yelled Maldeor, but it was too late. The damaged pillars wobbled and collapsed. Whole icicles fell down, and the ceiling caved in. What had been beautiful was now deadly. A chilling tune filled the room as the ice fell onto the floor. The archaeopteryxes were trapped. Seeing Maldeor distracted, the penguin scholar wriggled from his grasp and escaped.

"This is a trap, a trick!" Maldeor shouted to his soldiers as wind from the sky blew upon them from a gaping hole in the roof. He hurriedly assembled his carriage and harnessed the geese. "Upward! Upward! Don't waste time fighting the penguins! Upward and northward, to Kauria immediately!" His knights and soldiers abandoned the fighting and hurried to follow him. Soon, the remaining archaeopteryxes and the geese were on the move again.

"They're going to Kauria. We must try to stop them!" Winger cried to Fleydur.

Gwendeleine nodded. "But they shall not be speedy. The food in their bellies will drag them down, and the water on their wings will stiffen. Their wings will feel like lead. There seems to be some fog gathering too. Hurry and you may fly ahead of them yet! Farewell, my friends. Thank you and good luck! Without you, many penguins might not be alive now!"

"Farewell! Keep your gemstone safe!" the eagle and the woodpecker cried back. Then, swinging up into the fog, the two birds flew north.

Wind-voice wasn't sure how far the wind had carried him. For the last several minutes he had been flying through a bundle of fog so thick he could not see the water below him or the dying evening sun ahead. But now the mist was thinning around him. He broke through the last few shreds of cloud to find himself over a sea that seemed endless, sprinkled with icy white islands. Far away, in the blue-black water, his eye caught a glimpse of green.

Yet there was something bright, much closer—two birds, one large, one small, flying furiously as they broke

free of another thick band of fog not far away. The smaller bird had a bright red head. Wind-voice heard, very faintly, the chiming of bells.

The sun dazzled Fleydur's and Winger's eyes as they dove through the last clinging shreds of fog. They hovered for a moment, trying to get their bearings. Winger blinked as something white flashed against the background of darkening evening sky. He gasped.

"I'm so glad you're alive!" Winger shouted as the three

friends fluttered around one another in midair. Delight and astonishment were close to making them dizzy.

Wind-voice seemed larger than the woodpecker had remembered. Fleydur swooped around, his bells jangling joyfully.

"Where is Stormac?" Winger suddenly whispered, though he understood at once when he saw the strawberry charm around Wind-voice's neck. They hovered still, in the air. In a trembling voice Wind-voice told the sad tale. He slowly took off the charm and held it out to Winger.

The woodpecker reached out his bamboolike claws and touched the wooden berry delicately. Two shining pearls of tears spilled down his face and onto the worn red wood. His eyes stared at the sea below.

"We've come this far, with a sea storm lifting our wings. We've traveled over desert, forest, ocean, with a storm of purpose and worry giving us determination. Pray, where is our own storm, to lift our hearts?" Then he recited softly,

O ye great pounding waves
Of this sorrowful sea
How much of thee
Are tears?

He sniffed and nodded his head jerkily, then handed the berry back to Wind-voice.

Fleydur bowed his head. Without a word, he took out a small sack. From it he scooped out the last of the tinsel stars that Stormac had loved so much.

He tossed them into the sky. "Stormac!" he bellowed. The silvery stars looked magical as they shimmered and scattered in the wind. "A valiant warrior. A valiant death."

"Stormac!" Wind-voice stared at the sparkles. He felt the grief shake him all over again. "It was at the island where he died that I found a clue from an alliance of seabirds: 'Find flowers amid ice.' Fleydur, we met your tribe, too. 'Look into the eyes to choose your path,' that's their clue."

"My family!" Fleydur looked scared and excited at the same time. He could find no other words to say.

"Wind-voice, we also found two other gems!" Winger exclaimed. "The robin's ruby said, 'What you love most is the key.' The penguins have a light blue Leasorn. It says, 'Find the bird who flies through waters.' "

Wind-voice shook his head. "They must point to the sword. But I don't understand what they mean."

"The penguins told us that there's an island with

green nearby," Fleydur said. "It's probably Kauria. We must take to our wings. The archaeopteryxes might have spotted it already. We can't stay here any longer."

The three friends stretched their wings and headed for Kauria.

Before long, Ewingerale was faltering. His wings ached with each beat. Wind-voice flew up under him. "Rest on my back a few minutes," he murmured.

"You're tired too," Winger whispered. "You can't carry me."

"I can do it." Wind-voice caught up to Fleydur. The two tried to fly steadily. Winger could feel the body heat of Wind-voice as his friend silently strained. The wind blew in their faces, pelting them with tiny, sharp flakes of ice and swirling a mist around them. Whiteness blotted out the world for a moment. When it cleared, Winger let out a sharp cry. "An army ahead of us!"

He pointed at a moving mass. The wind had seized a banner that a bird in the vanguard was carrying. It was blue in the darkening sky, and on it was a mountain peak and a black cloud split by a lightning bolt.

"Skythunder," Fleydur cried, astonished.

"It's your brother!" Wind-voice exclaimed. "It's Forlath. He said he'd bring help." He peered more closely at the far-off mass of birds and made out flashes of color—the bright red wings of parrots, and white and gray that might be seagulls. Did he even catch a glimpse of a heron's long yellow legs?

"But how—" Fleydur said. "But why—"

"No time now!" shouted Wind-voice. Behind them, the archaeopteryx army broke out of a cloud and flapped closer. Wind-voice realized the enemy had spotted them and had changed course to intercept them. He and his companions would be trapped. But from the mass of gray archaeopteryx feathers and bright steel, a single bird pointed a sword, not toward Forlath's army, nor toward Wind-voice but toward something that had been obscured by a stray layer of mist that hung over the sea.

"Maldeor." Wind-voice shuddered.

What separates a hero from a villain?
Now I understand.
—from "Ewingerale's Diary,"
in the Old Scripture

16
CROSSING SWORDS

The woodpecker and the eagle! No, eagles . . ."
Maldeor crouched on the edge of his carriage,
ready to launch himself. He turned to Kawaka.
"Those sniveling Skythunder hook-beaks have finally
come out of hiding. Ha, golden eagles fighting over
water! Ridiculous. Sir Kawaka, attack them!"

Maldeor gargled one last beakful of medicine and
leaped down.

All around, the two armies clashed together in one turbulent cloud that rained feathers and blood. Before Maldeor could fly farther, an arrow fell toward him. It went right through his magical wing, but the vaporous wing did not seem to heal as quickly.

He looked back. Ewingerale, Fleydur, and Wind-voice surrounded him. "Not dead? Not blind?" Maldeor gasped at the sight of Wind-voice, who was much bigger than before. *Calm down, Maldeor,* he said silently to himself. *Fight the weakest one first, and get rid of them one by one.* Maldeor swung his sword at Ewingerale. Within a few moves, the woodpecker tumbled, and the first gust of wind sent him falling. *The eagle next,* Maldeor thought, and turned.

Wind-voice dived down to rescue Winger. "I'm all right," the woodpecker murmured.

"Fleydur, come here and help!" Wind-voice shouted, but when he looked back, he saw the eagle veering in a circle, defeated by Maldeor as well.

"Now you!" Maldeor cried. "One on one."

Fleydur recovered and went to tend Winger while Wind-voice rose up in the air to face his enemy. *What? He's much more skilled than he seems . . . I can't waste time parrying him when there's only a few hours left to Hero's Day.* Maldeor abruptly turned and dove down toward the shroud of mist.

"No!" Wind-voice cried. *I must stop him.* He followed where Maldeor had gone. The mist swallowed him. "So this is Kauria," he said to himself as an island, sandy yellow and fringed with green, appeared below. *Find flowers amid ice,* Wind-voice thought. This was what the first clue had meant.

Wind-voice swooped lower. The island was bird-shaped. Long sandy beaches stretched out on either side; it looked as if the bird were soaring through the dark blue ocean. *Find the bird who flies through waters.* The gems indeed held the clues he needed. "Oh, Stormac," he whispered, thinking of the skeptical myna. "You should be here to see this."

The sea wind swept him inland. A clue suddenly leaped into his mind. *The eye of the bird sees your wish.* He aimed for the part of the island shaped like a bird's head. A steep gray cliff formed the beak. He hovered toward where the bird's eye should be. Suddenly a pyramid appeared there magically, in the middle of the sandy waste.

Wind-voice felt all the feathers on his neck rise. He charged at a small gate set in the side of the pyramid just in time to see a tail, gray and feathered, disappear inside.

Wind-voice dove through the empty doorway and into a long, narrow tunnel. He soared down the stone corridor.

He was in a great round hall. There were towering panels of stained glass standing on all sides but no sign of Maldeor. Where had he gone? Wind-voice hurried down the hall, peering around him. As he passed the first

panel, a candle behind it burst into flame, making him jump back. It showed a finch, dying, crushed beneath the claws of a huge archaeopteryx who, laughing, held a long sword.

Cruel scenes blazed out from each panel as Wind-voice passed by. But still there was no sign of Maldeor.

There was only one panel still dark. As Wind-voice

dashed past it, the image on it glowed with brilliant color. Wind-voice stopped, hesitated, and came back to look.

The panel showed a group of hopeful birds—a robin, a kingfisher, a penguin, an eagle, a seagull, a parrot—reaching their claws out. Above their heads hovered gemstones.

As Wind-voice stared, the glass window split and opened like a door.

Inside was a tunnel that curved up and out of his sight. He launched himself forward and pumped his wings for height. The smooth, rounded walls of the tunnel were covered by a smooth white surface, like mother-of-pearl, that gave off its own light so he could see where he was going. The tunnel spiraled, taking him higher and higher. One wing tip lightly brushed the outer wall as he flew faster and faster. The turns were tight but the slope was not steep.

Then he heard vibrating booms inside. They got louder as Wind-voice flew higher.

The tunnel abruptly ended and he nearly ran into the back of the archaeopteryx, hovering, staring at a solid flat wall, a dead end, before him. On the wall hung a carving of gray feldspar. Concentric rings went dizzyingly around a central point, where two flat rocks twice the size of Maldeor overlapped each other. Maldeor jerked his head up at the sound of Wind-voice's panting.

His eyes widened momentarily. Wind-voice was now the same size as he was!

"Trying to stop me, are you? Seeking death?" he snarled. He drew his sword and dove at Wind-voice.

Wind-voice flew to one wall, braced himself against it, pushed off, and leaped to the left. He kept his sword between himself and Maldeor. He must distract him and buy time for the hero to arrive and claim the sword.

"There's something I don't understand," he heard himself saying. "How can you wage such war and yet say that you want to bring peace?"

Maldeor snorted as if it were obvious. "I will make a better world, free of ignoramuses and meaningless fighting, where birds have common sense, like me." *Better kill him off immediately now when he has little room to escape,* Maldeor thought. The archaeopteryx unleashed his ultimate move, the Deadly Fate. Wind-voice met it with a vertical slash. His cheek and neck burned and he felt blood beneath his eye. Otherwise he was unharmed.

Maldeor stared at Wind-voice. "You ought to have died! Slave you have been; though you've grown in size, now you bear such a mark again." Maldeor laughed, trying to cover his confusion. "And you have a slave's stupidity, too, or you would understand the obvious. Peace can only be gained by force. Birds must be controlled. There is no other way."

"Peace cannot be forced," Wind-voice retorted firmly. "There is no true peace under force."

Maldeor's face was a picture of derision and contempt. He slashed out again, but Wind-voice parried successfully. The clang of the steel blades rang and echoed off the close stone walls.

Where was the hero? Surely he would come any moment now. Wind-voice knew he could not hold out for long. "When the hero comes," he murmured. "When he comes . . ."

"He is here," Maldeor said. "I am he. How does this door open?" Maldeor demanded. "You wouldn't have come here unless you thought you could open it. Tell me and perhaps I'll let you live!"

Wind-voice retreated until the stone wall was at his back, and Maldeor swooped in closer. Wind-voice could see a vein pulsating on the archaeopteryx's left eyelid like a small azure snake.

"I don't know!" Wind-voice shot back. *Peace opens the door*, he thought. *But what does that mean?* He folded his wings, dropping suddenly below Maldeor, and then rose up beneath him. Maldeor screeched with rage and struggled to turn in the narrow space. Now Wind-voice was nearer to the mysterious door than his enemy was. But when he tried to lay a claw upon it, something unseen but too powerful to be resisted seemed to brush him aside.

All of a sudden, something clicked in Wind-voice's mind. To get through that door, he must not be armed. He must go in peace.

He looked back. Maldeor was growling at him now. Would he be crazy to disarm himself when he was a mere wing's length away from a murderer?

The hero wasn't here, and if he let Maldeor kill him, the archaeopteryx might easily figure out how to open the door, and then the sword would be his.

Wind-voice dropped his weapon. It fell and clattered on the shining floor of the tunnel and started sliding, curving out of sight along the spiral.

A deep grinding noise shook the carving on the wall. The two flat rocks trembled and slowly slid apart to reveal a round gaping hole.

Maldeor understood at once. *I must disarm myself, but I won't let 013-Unidentified off so easily. . . .* Instead of dropping his weapon, he flung it at Wind-voice's head. As Wind-voice ducked to avoid the whirling blade,

Maldeor got a head start. He charged into the hole and disappeared.

"Oh no . . ." Worry gnawed at Wind-voice's heart. He immediately zipped into the hole as well. Blackness blanketed him. Nothing could be seen ahead. Where was Maldeor? The darkness lasted for a few seconds, and then unexpectedly two monstrous eyes lit up before them. *What's that?* Wind-voice wondered. As he flew closer, he discovered that they were only eye-shaped crystal doors. "Look into the eyes to choose your path," Wind-voice said to himself.

A milky white mist swirled across the doors; then it cleared and on each crystal a scene appeared. Wind-voice saw himself raising a blazing sword in his claws on the right crystal. On the left crystal loomed ghostly, thin faces, all sorts of birds, ragged and dirty, with big eyes. They reached out their claws beseechingly.

"Which way did Maldeor go?" Wind-voice wondered. He looked at the image of the poor birds on the left. He pushed it and it swung inward.

The left door didn't lead to a room at all but into a deep green forest. Above was a clouded sky. A shining light low in the mid-distance caught Wind-voice's attention. "A fallen star," he whispered, and drifted toward it.

But the light spilled from a crystal casket, caught in the twining boughs of an oddly shaped tree. The sheer intensity of the light made the casket glow like a white cylinder.

Where is the hero? Where is Maldeor? Wind-voice thought. *Since the hero's sword is here, and since Maldeor is near, Maldeor could get the sword at any moment. I'll stay here and fight him if he does. But what if I lose? I must take the sword out and hide it somewhere for the hero so that Maldeor cannot find it.*

A golden disk remained visible where the keyhole should have been. At the very center a heart had been etched, so painstakingly detailed, it seemed to throb in the flickering light. Seven round, clear stones were inlaid in a circle around it. A miniature object was suspended in each stone: a ruler's crown, two crossed swords, a treasure chest, a bird holding a green sprig, a rose, a book, a grass nest. *What you love most is the key,* Wind-voice said to himself.

Suddenly a deep, rich voice echoed out of the darkness. *"You have only one choice."* Wind-voice turned around, but there was nobird. Mystified, he looked down again at the stones.

A crown ... ruling, he thought. *I certainly don't want to control others.* His eyes fell lower. *The two swords together could only mean battle, and battle is cruel. Then the treasure chest? With riches, a bird can help the poor . . .* he thought, and hesitated before continuing. *The bird with the branch is the only image that contains an animal.* He hesitated again, longer this time. *The rose might mean love; the book, learning; and the nest, family . . . All of those are surely important.* Wind-voice swayed in a second of indecision. He looked back up again, and his eyes stayed on the stone of the bird with the branch. *It looks like an olive branch. It must mean peace,* he thought. *How can families stay together and survive in the cruelty of battle? Aren't books destroyed in war? Even if there were books, how could fighting birds have the time to read them? War is synonymous with death. Can riches stop any of it? No. To have love, learning, and family, peace must come first. I care about peace,* he thought. He raised a foot and pressed the stone with the bird holding the olive branch.

Though it was only a click, in the echoing forest it sounded like a loud clattering bang as the casket opened, the lid slowly rising and swinging back.

The voice spoke again. *"This is the hero's sword."*

How often had Wind-voice thought about the sword since the first time he had heard of it from Fisher?

The beauty of it was its pure, strong simplicity—it was long and straight like a ray of sunshine. The ivory scabbard's designs of water and wind were clean and flowing; the bold curves on the dragonlike hilt seemed alive. The source of all the light was the Leasorn gemstone embedded in the hilt. A living rainbow seemed to swirl inside.

"How can I make sure Maldeor doesn't get the sword?" asked Wind-voice.

"*There is only one way. You must use the strength of your heart to seal the casket from evil. This is a sacrifice. Are you willing?*"

Wind-voice gazed at the sword. Then he closed his eyes. He could almost see the figure of his mother in the sunshine. His memory was blurred by time, but Wind-voice

tried to bring the picture into focus. Then, in the background, a lost heron drifted into view. "*He made the most beautiful candles,*" Aredrem whispered. "*Even ones of heron chicks . . . it's a pity, but they've all burned out now . . .*"

Appearing out of the darkness, Winger spoke. "*I am*

an orphan. With my eyes, I have seen the deaths of my mother, father, and sister."

Then Forlath's voice rang out. *"Fleydur let himself be disowned by his family, where he was a prince, so that he could bring joy to war-stricken birds."*

At last Stormac's voice carried to him, again telling Wind-voice his regret. *"I was like the fool who flew through a rain cloud, thinking it was cream, and came out wet on the other side."*

Wind-voice opened his eyes. "Yes," he whispered. "How shall I do it?"

"All you need to do is to place your right claw on your heart."

Somehow, the figures of his mother, Irene, Ewingerale, Fleydur, Stormac, and Aredrem seemed to linger in the corners of his eyes, waiting. *Why isn't the hero here?* he wondered. Facing the sword, he raised his claw slowly and pressed it on his chest, next to Stormac's strawberry. *Thump-thump . . . thump-thump . . .* His heartbeat filled his ears, faster and faster, louder and louder. With each loud pound, the crystal lid moved. The lid swung closed with a click. Before his eyes, the casket, the sword, and the shining light disappeared.

There was only a swirl of dark mist where it had been. The distant tolls of a silver bell—*dong . . . dong . . .*

dong—sounded the time of midnight. Hero's Day had ended. Wind-voice took a deep breath and looked around at the empty, misty forest.

There was nothing more for him to do.

He took off, flew past vines and branches, landed, and then trudged slowly, tiredly back to the milky crystal door. Laboriously he pulled it open. Like a fire-stunned moth he fluttered back into the dark hall, just in time to see the right chamber's door swing open and a figure rush out. A small source of light illuminated Maldeor's gloating face, long, ragged shadows blotching below his hooded eyes and neck, further distorting them.

The archaeopteryx held a glowing golden sword aloft.

Is there another hero's sword? Wind-voice was horror-stricken.

"You fool!" Maldeor laughed maniacally. "I've got the hero's sword. It was waiting for me to take it. You've got nothing . . . nothing but death! Grown even bigger, have you? I'll test the magic of this sword on you first!" Shrieking with glee, he propelled himself toward Wind-voice, who was unarmed.

The darkness around them seemed to *whoosh* in surprise. Pinpricks of light flared up all around them. They were not in a dark stretch of nothingness but in a magnificent hall with pillars soaring to the ceiling and twenty-four torches lined up on each side.

The archaeopteryx raised his sword with his claws and cleaved down mightily.

Wind-voice ducked with a nimble spin to the left. As the torchlights turned into streaks in his vision, he felt a warm, certain glow in his heart. Something solid materialized in his claws. He gripped it instinctively and brought it up in an underclaw as he snapped out of his spin. The torchlights all jumped higher.

The object in his claws clashed with Maldeor's sword. The archaeopteryx *caw*ed with surprise. Wind-voice looked down at what he was holding, but he only saw a whitish rod that faded away again.

Angered, Maldeor attacked again and again, and the strange rod reappeared each time so that Wind-voice was able to block each blow. Every fifteen minutes, a torch burned out, and they clanged all over the hall, till only eight torches were left.

Working himself into a rage of frenzied frustration, Maldeor raised his sword and started hacking down again and again, moving forward. The rod shimmered and shook as the blows rained down upon it.

Where are you, hero? Wind-voice thought. He closed

his eyes. Then all of a sudden a great burst of energy swelled his heart. He let it run down his leg, to his foot, to the rod he was holding. Maldeor's sword crashed down on it.

Maldeor screamed. Wind-voice opened his eyes to see the rod solidify into something familiar, and the ivory sheath of the true hero's sword shattered into a thousand pieces. The shards flew all around him, but none fell on him because the hero's sword was in his claws. A sudden brightness blazed from the bare blade.

There had never been two hero's swords. There was only one.

Maldeor felt a great pile of sand slipping through his claws as his sword crumbled and dissolved into dust. The ceiling above them shivered and cracked, letting in the early sunlight. Chunks of stone rained down.

*This is the most magnificent day
in the history of all birds.*
—FROM "EWINGERALE'S DIARY,"
IN THE OLD SCRIPTURE

17
HERO

Under a round, bright moon, one of the most important battles of birdkind was taking place.

"Let us form a twin for the moon!" Ewingerale cried.

Forlath echoed him, sending the message far and wide with his bellow. In the midst of murmurings and shouts, Fleydur raised a silver trumpet that his brother had just given him and blew to the stars.

As the bell tolled midnight, scarlet macaws, green parrots, petrels, gulls, black-browed albatrosses, and the golden eagles linked wingtips in the night sky, hovering in a gigantic dome around the pyramid. The edges of flashing wings were gilded silver by the moonlight. "We may not hold them forever," Forlath said. "But for the sake of a better future, we shall try!"

With vulgar screams erupting in waves, the archaeopteryxes fell on them, their yellowish eyeballs and teeth catching the light, their filthy brown-and-khaki uniforms making them look like a stream of mud. The battle raged on, minute by minute, hour by hour.

Despite the seabirds' agility, the eagles' strength, and the parrots' alertness, by the time the sun appeared above the ocean, they were faltering. "Come to us, hero," Winger whispered.

Then a rumbling shook the ground beneath the armies and sent tremors into the air. Two swords shot out of a chute on the side of the pyramid. One was Maldeor's old sword, and the other was Wind-voice's. The battling birds paused, looking down to see the pyramid tumble into rubble.

"What's happening? Is the hero dead?" Murmurings traveled from one beak to another. The archaeopteryxes lingered in the air, calling for their emperor.

Birds backed away. Stunned, Winger fluttered forward. A great cloud of dust rose from the ruin. Shafts of sunlight streamed through it, and the golden dust looked beautiful.

"Wind-voice," Ewingerale called. Had the white bird gone into the pyramid? Had he been crushed by the falling stones? "Oh, Wind-voice, no . . ."

Then a small figure flew up through the sun-spangled cloud of dust, almost glowing in the golden light.

"The hero!" one archaeopteryx cheered, and others took up the cry. "The hero! Hail thee, great Ancient Wing!"

The figure spread its wings wide. They flashed white. He held a sword in his claws.

The hero wasn't Maldeor, Ewingerale realized. It had never been Maldeor.

It was Wind-voice.

Blazing light burst out from the sword in the white bird's grip. It spread across the battlefield. Swords and spears of the archaeopteryxes shimmered brightly as if in response and then began to glow as if they had just come from the forge. Maldeor's army flung their hot weapons to the ground. Panic spread among the archaeopteryxes. Scrambling in the air, squawking with fright and dismay, they turned and fled.

Wind-voice alighted on the ground, looking stunned. He hopped slowly down the fallen pyramid toward Winger, from one rock to another, his sword held so loosely that the glowing blade almost dragged in the sand. Silence prevailed.

When he reached the woodpecker, he stopped. Winger's red head and the curved tip of the harp on his back stood out in the gentle haze of dust. The two looked at each other. Then the woodpecker said "Oh, Wind-voice!"

Something in the woodpecker's voice caused Wind-voice to turn around. He gasped. The path he had just walked was marked by a lush line of green, for the dead vines that had once curled in the sand had sprung to life, their heart-shaped leaves unfurling at the touch of his dragging sword. Green, that splendid color, was filling the barren desert around them, almost blinding their dazzled eyes. Wind-voice looked down at his sword, amazed.

He raised it slowly and pointed it at a withered olive tree. With a *whoosh* like a faint breeze, buds popped out of the dry branches and tiny fruit sprang forth. Smiling now, Wind-voice whirled his sword and pointed to the ground. The sand melted into rich brown earth; grass sprang from it and flowers opened, turning their faces to the brilliant sun. He flicked his claws, and where the sword pointed, the ground suddenly split open and a river flowed out.

Then he raised the sword high in the air.

White light was all they could see.

When they recovered, they found themselves in a green, dense jungle.

Wind-voice looked in amazement at the sword in his claws. "I—I'll keep it safe," he muttered to Winger. "For the hero, when he comes . . ."

Winger was smiling a light, dreamy smile that radiated all over his thin face. "The hero is here, Wind-voice," he said, awed. "You're the hero."

"Hero . . ." Fleydur, Forlath, and the rest of the rebel army landed in a circle around Wind-voice. A wave of greetings surrounded him. "Show us the way, hero," somebird cried. Everybird looked at Wind-voice, waiting for him to do something. Wind-voice glanced around. He noticed a small break in the dense jungle—a path.

He flapped toward it. For some reason, he knew it was the right way. "Follow me, friends," he called. Together, Wind-voice, Ewingerale, Fleydur, Forlath, and their army flew along the path to a magnificent castle, the walls of which were living trees linked together.

Standing at the gate was a golden figure. "You have healed our island," the phoenix king cried gratefully to Wind-voice. Toucans and birds of paradise surrounded them. "We have waited three years for your coming! So has birdkind. Look!"

On the horizon, thousands of birds were arriving to

witness the awesome arrival of the hero. Those who could not fly were riding on the backs of those who could or were arriving in hot-air balloons. Birds were swimming, too, and some even sailed there in boats. Hour after hour, more birds flooded Kauria.

At noon the ceremony began.

As Wind-voice stood on a balcony listening to Pepheroh's words carrying to the birds who'd come from far and wide, a thought that had buzzed persistently around his head like a bee bothered him again. Maldeor had said that birds fell into two categories: good and evil. For a time Wind-voice had wondered if that might be true . . . but . . .

No, the world was not split distinctly like two wings on a bird: white and black, good and evil. There was gray, plenty of it—like Dubto, caught between his compassion and his loyalty; like the eagles of Skythunder, who thought it was right to disown their own prince; like Stormac, brave and loyal, but fighting the weakness that had, in the end, taken him to his death. Perhaps even like Maldeor. Wind-voice felt calmer then, as if he had passed a test.

Indeed, life is full of tests, he thought. *You don't know what they are, so you must treat everything in life with the same care you would bring to a test on which your future rests. I realize that the most important test of all,* Wind-voice marveled, *in my quest, and perhaps in every bird's quest, is the test to be the master of fate.*

"Wind-voice." Pepheroh called gently to him.

He turned to face the phoenix, bowed deeply, and knelt down. In his claws he held the sword, offering it to the king. The phoenix grasped the hilt. He held the sword solemnly before him, and the birds below were quiet. Wind-voice opened his left wing. King Pepheroh ran the flat of the blade slowly along it. The metal felt cool and heavy. "May your heart be strong and true, forever passing on the meaning of love and friendship," the phoenix said.

Wind-voice spread his right wing. The blade stroked it as well. "May your mind be brave and just, forever showing us the importance of peace and freedom. Now rise," murmured the king, and then louder so that everybird could hear: "Rise!" His old, fatherly face broke into a deep smile, and he held the sword out to Wind-voice. Wind-voice closed his claws slowly around the hilt. They turned to face the sea of silent birds, and Pepheroh firmly wrapped his own claws around Wind-voice's. They raised them high so that all could see the light glinting off the blade. Pepheroh called out, "From now on, Wind-voice shall be also known as Swordbird!"

"Swordbird! Swordbird! Swordbird!" Wave after wave of deafening cheers rose.

Wind-voice stood there, dazed. A choking joy mingled with a deep gratitude filled his whole being. Such an honor it was, to be given the responsibility of caring for birdkind.

"Thank you. There are heroes all among us. Without many birds, I might not have achieved this today. I want to thank my companions, Winger the woodpecker and Fleydur the eagle, for their support, poems, and songs. I want to thank Stormac the myna"—Wind-voice touched the berry charm around his neck—"who was like a brother to me. I want to thank Fisher, Rhea, Kari, Gwendeleine, and the birds of their tribe for their help and care, and I want to thank all of you here. I also want to thank my mother, Irene. I don't know who my father is, though—"

"Perhaps your father is the Great Spirit," said Pepheroh, smiling.

"Then I want to thank the Great Spirit too." Wind-voice gazed into the sky. He took a deep breath. He addressed everybird. "We are all heroes. One hero isn't enough. We must all take care of one another." A new wave of applause traveled from one end of the crowd to the other. Birds fluttered together in the sky, forming the words "Peace," "Freedom," "Love," and "Justice."

He had started this—this nightmare, this dream, the journey, this . . . quest—as a muddled youngster, weak, wanting only to escape violence and servitude. Yet instead he had unexpectedly found glowing treasures— Stormac's wooden berry, Winger's harp, Fleydur's songs. He had found his place. He had found himself.

Closing his eyes, he heard snatches of conversation from a long time ago:

"When is this hero coming?"

"Soon, soon."

He opened his eyes, smiled, and saw thousands of birds cheering before him. The hero was ready now.

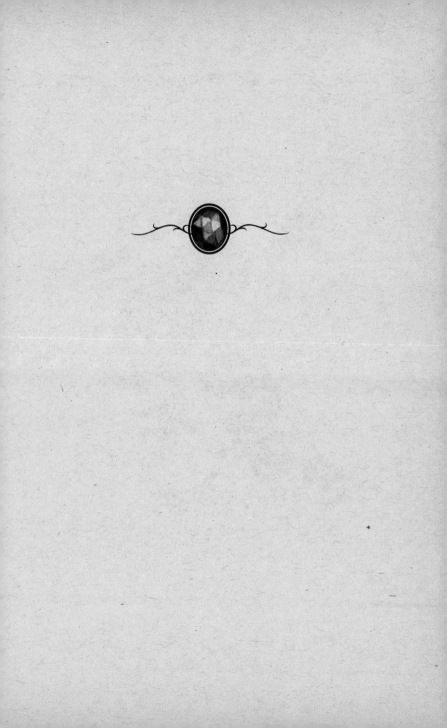

18
EXCERPT FROM EWINGERALE'S DIARY

—EXCERPT FROM PAGE 341 OF
"EWINGERALE'S DIARY" IN THE OLD SCRIPTURE

Early fall, Day of Remembrance

Ever since Hero's Day, Swordbird has become world famous.

As I strum my claws across the strings of my harp, I seem to hear the world laughing with me. Would you believe that every day now, weapons are melted down to be formed into flutes, telescopes, pen nibs, and even bells? Ever since Swordbird, our hero, came two seasons ago, more birds have discarded their axes, swords, and spears to hold books instead.

"You know," Kari the macaw said to me some time ago, "the Avish words on our green gemstone shone brightly the moment Wind-voice held the true hero's sword. Then the words disappeared!" As I traveled about, other tribes confirmed this phenomenon. She told me that birds, singing the "Song of Swordbird," could now use the Leasorn gems as a link to call Swordbird to come.

What happened to the remaining archaeopteryx army and their battalions? Leaderless, they fought among themselves and, at last, in a huff, scattered into small bands. The same fate awaited their allies, the pirates and the outlaw crows, ravens, and mynas. Some retreated into remote haunts, some tried more devilry, but a few changed their ways and befriended us.

As for Wind-voice, I only saw him once in my dreams, after Hero's Day. He said to me, "Winger, my mortal self did die when the pyramid crashed down. I understand now. I sacrificed myself so that I, as a spirit, can forever guard peace and freedom, and I'm glad."

So am I. Even though my heart clenches when I think

of Wind-voice, a calm, earnest joy enfolds me when I think of the brighter era awaiting birdkind.

"You've written so much of our quest in your diary," Wind-voice said. "I hope you will finish writing all of it."

"I think I shall," I replied.

As Wind-voice rescues and helps in the sky, we do our best on the earth. Fleydur, accepted back by his family, has many young budding musicians following him. Kari the macaw and her teacher, Rhea the shrike, travel together, teaching the art of healing. As for me— well, following Wind-voice's suggestion, I have been happily busy organizing the account in my diary of all that happened in the days I traveled with him. The good phoenix king, Pepheroh, printed it in a book called the *Old Scripture*. It also contains the "Song of Swordbird," which is used to call Swordbird. We will send out copies to everybird so that all birds may know what we have gone through, learn from our experience, and live peacefully.

Sometimes we companions gather on the islands of the seabirds to pay our respects to Stormac. A clear spring now gushes where he was buried, as if by magic. Even though it is so remote from the Marshes, somehow the water has the sweet taste of the cedar trees that grow in the myna's homeland. It is here that we recall the past.

We have agreed on one thing: With the powers of pen, song, and healing, we can help make the world a better place.

Swordbird bless us all!

—*Winger*

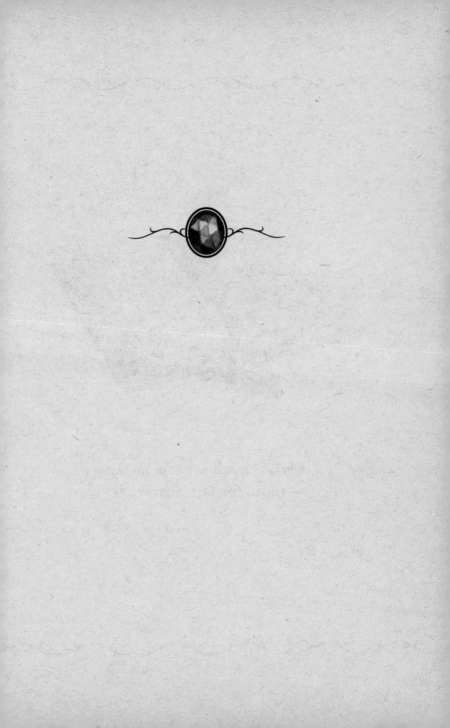

A hero's heart is as vast as the sky.
—FROM THE OLD SCRIPTURE

The First Bright Moon Festival

It was spring.

Kauria was in bloom. Though it was hidden in mists from the rest of the world, for some reason, on the night of the first anniversary of Hero's Day, birds found it without difficulty.

Flocks of birds were gathered there—some young, some old, some who had never been there before, some who had, some who were descendants of heroes, some who had met or traveled with Wind-voice. It didn't matter who they were; they were all there for the same purpose.

All gazed into the sky. The moon was round, like a mirror of dreams, and as they stood, they seemed to see and hear things. Like an echo from a year ago, they heard cheerings: "Swordbird! Swordbird!"

There was the faint strum of a harp, and then Ewingerale walked in among them. He started singing:

> *On our sword quest we have learned that*
> *Fate is wind, not a river.*
> *The directions of wind can always change*
> *But rivers shall flow the same.*
> *No matter which way the wind shall blow,*
> *Dare to use your wings.*

Fleydur the eagle came striding from the other side, singing melodiously:

> *On our sword quest we have learned*
> *The reason why we come to this world.*
> *Not for fighting, not for taking,*
> *But for living, and for giving.*
> *Not merely for eating and sleeping day after day,*
> *But for flying toward lofty goals.*

Ewingerale continued the song:

> *On our sword quest we have learned that*
> *True happiness is built upon dedication.*
> *A grass nest woven by ourselves*
> *Outshines a palace inherited,*
> *Crabapples foraged from a bush*
> *Taste sweeter than stolen oranges.*

Fleydur sang joyously:

> *On our sword quest we have learned to*
> *Value the world the way we value our family.*
> *If we spread kindness wherever we go,*
> *Then we have thousands of brothers and sisters.*
> *Loving and caring brightens our world.*
> *They bring us closer to the Great Spirit.*

The two friends stood side by side, faces to the moon, and sang the last words together:

> *To live is to treasure everything.*
> *To live is to strive*
> *For tomorrow*
> *And for a bright future.*

And then, in a soft chorus, the crowd of birds sang a song written by Ewingerale, who is now the scribe, and Fleydur, now the bard of the eagles.

O joy be on the day of the Bright Moon Festival
Holy day of Swordbird's birth,
A day when birds sing and dance,
And when a round, bright moon shines on the earth . . .

Somewhere among them, somebird whispered, "Happy birthday, Swordbird."

It was indeed a magical night, and perhaps it was the excitement, perhaps it was a trick of the light, or perhaps it was real . . .

For Swordbird's figure seemed to glide across the moon, his graceful wings saluting a peaceful world.

Major Characters

AQUAL—tern, the chief of the Qua, the seabirds' alliance.

AREDREM—great blue heron, wife of Fisher.

DUBTO—archaeopteryx, soldier of the Marshes Battalion of the archaeopteryx army.

EWINGERALE (WINGER)—red-bellied woodpecker, companion of Wind-voice, harpist, and primary author of the *Old Scripture*.

FISHER—great blue heron, leader of the rebel group of the Marshes territory.

FLEYDUR—golden eagle; son of Morgan, king of Skythunder; brother of Forlath; companion of Wind-voice; wandering bard.

FORLATH—golden eagle; son of Morgan, king of Skythunder; brother of Fleydur.

GREAT SPIRIT—creator of the earth and birdkind.

GWENDELEINE—emperor penguin, lady of the Illagoo tribe.

HUNGRIAS—archaeopteryx, the Ancient Wing, and emperor of archaeopteryxes; killed by Maldeor.

IRENE—dove, mother of Wind-voice.

KARI—scarlet macaw, friend of Wind-voice, healer, member of the Half-moon tribe.

KAWAKA—archaeopteryx, leader of the Marshes Battalion of the archaeopteryx army, later head knight of the Royal Court, brother of Rattle-bones.

MALDEOR—archaeopteryx, former head knight of the Royal Court, succeeded Hungrias as the Ancient Wing and emperor of archaeopteryxes, author of the *Book of Heresy*.

MORGAN—golden eagle, king of Skythunder, father of Fleydur and Forlath.

PEPHEROH—phoenix, king of Kauria, the magical Island of Paradise.

PHAËTHON—archaeopteryx, prince of the archaeopteryx empire, son of Hungrias.

RAG-FOOT—brown skua, captain of the pirates of the Pearls Archipelago.

RATTLE-BONES—archaeopteryx, knight of the Royal Court, brother of Kawaka.

RHEA—shrike, healer who hosted a rebel meeting.

STORMAC—hill myna, companion of Wind-voice.

SWORDBIRD (WIND-VOICE)—white bird, guardian of peace, son of the Great Spirit.

WIND-VOICE—the same as Swordbird.

WINGER—the same as Ewingerale.

YAMA—supreme evil spirit who is the opposite of the Great Spirit.

YIN SOUL—half-ghost of a four-winged dinosaur who wanted to be reincarnated.

ACKNOWLEDGMENTS

Many writers believe that to write a novel, especially a fantasy novel, is to go on a quest. At fourteen, I feel lucky to have experienced two quests. During them, many people helped and encouraged me. I am deeply grateful to them.

First, I would like to thank Ms. Phoebe Yeh, editorial director of HarperCollins Children's Books. Through my frequent contact with her, I feel that she has become my dear teacher and lifelong friend. She sets her whole mind and heart on her work, which makes me realize that once you have found something you love to do, you are always energetic. Without her meticulous guidance and help, none of my quests could have been completed.

Profound thanks to Ms. Jane Friedman, president and CEO of HarperCollins, Worldwide, one of the most powerful and broadminded people I've ever met. It is she who gave me wings to fly in the sky of the literature world. She has not only encouraged me, but she also encourages kids all over the world to read and write. Thousands of emails to me from young writers reflect this.

I would also like to thank many other HarperCollins people: Ms. Susan Katz, president and publisher of HarperCollins Children's Books, for sending me a delightful bird book that, to me, is much more than a book; Ms. Kate Jackson, senior vice president of HarperCollins Children's Books, for her great expectations of me; Ms. Joan Rosen, vice president and director of subsidiary rights; Ms. Audra Boltion, associate director of publicity; Ms. Mary Albi, director of marketing; Mr. Greg Ferguson, assistant editor; and Ms. Amy Ryan, art supervisor, for their enthusiastic support and constant help; Ms. Colleen Delany, for performing the story so vividly in the audio book of *Swordbird*; and Mr. Mark Zug and Ms. Jo-Anne Rioux for their wonderful artwork that made *Sword Quest* come alive.

My heartfelt thanks also go to Ms. Stella Chou, managing director for HarperCollins Chinese Business Development, and Ms. Michelle Wu, Marketing and Communications Manager, for shepherding the Chinese bilingual edition of *Sword Quest*.

During my own quest of writing and traveling, teachers and friends either read my manuscript or supported me with kindness. I would like to thank Dr. Linda Lamme, professor of children's literature—I was overjoyed to hear her sensible advice on what makes a children's book good; **Ms. Jennifer Wise, my sunny middle-school principal, for encouraging all the students in my school to write by sharing my story with them; and Ms. Diane Anding, Ms. Jennifer Diley, Ms. Stephanie Leander, Ms. Maria Olsen, and Ms. Elizabeth Freeman, my amazing eighth-grade teachers.**

As I wrote *Sword Quest*, I had the good fortune to visit my alma mater. It was like a homecoming! I want to thank Mr. Barry Guinn and Ms. Debbie Geiss, two of the most warmhearted principals I've ever known; my phenomenal former teachers Ms. Melissa Barnello and Ms. Judy Allen, for their wonderful teaching and cordial support; Mr. Timothy Simmons and Mr. Ben Farstad, my cool third-grade teachers; Ms. Diane Goodwin, my earliest teacher of literature, whose appearance at a bookstore signing made me so happy that I was moved to tears; Ms. Betty Barr, MBE, for her precious comments and advice; Professor Nancy Hodes, who inspired me a lot; Professor Robert Loach, for his intercultural insights; Dr. John Cech, for offering me the opportunity to talk with a professor of children's literature on his radio program; Professor Hank Conner, for inviting me to be a guest speaker on his special program, "Conner Calling," and for his wit; the Audubon Society of Florida, for making me an honorary member and adopting a bald eagle in my name; Ms. Patricia Brigati, for turning on the lights of the first Christmas tree in my life;

Ms. Debbie O'Donnell and Ms. Jen Obermaier, librarians; and Ms. Catherine Tarbox and Ms. Joy Merrill, bookstore managers (there are many others; I cannot name them all), for inviting me to do presentations at my second home, libraries and bookstores.

Support from celebrities energized me while writing *Sword Quest*. I want to thank Mr. Jackie Chan, the martial arts movie star, for his encouragement; Ms. Martha Stewart, also a bird lover, for her unforgettable conversation with me; and Mr. Al Roker, who wrote to me: "Sunny skies always."

Family support is priceless. I remember when I was small, my grandparents bought lots of books for me and read them to me night after night. I would like to thank them, as well as my parents, who listened to my story of Wind-voice and gave me invaluable suggestions.

Of course, a chirp of thanks to my pet lovebirds, Pandora, Ever-sky, and Dyppler, the great blue heron in the pond across the street, and the resident red-shouldered hawk who often perches sagely on the bar of a swing just beyond my window.

It's good to meet people (and birds) and learn from them.

SWORD QUEST

The Author's Inspiration behind *Sword Quest*

I WROTE *SWORDBIRD* JUST for myself. Writing *Sword Quest* was a very different experience. I wrote *Sword Quest* for my readers and friends in order to satisfy their curiosity as well as my own.

The idea for writing *Swordbird* came from a dream; *Sword Quest* was inspired from an untold story in *Swordbird*. Readers kept asking me, "How did Wind-voice become Swordbird?" "Who wrote the *Old Scripture* and the *Book of Heresy*?" Yes, how did Wind-voice become Swordbird? I thought. Where did Wind-voice get his sword? How did Ewingerale the woodpecker play a part in Wind-voice's journey? This sounds like an exciting story that I must tell.

When I write stories, I like to explore something special, something that I've never seen or heard before. In this way, my writing becomes a process of discovery, challenging and thrilling. But finding that special something can be elusive. Sometimes it can take up countless days of deep thinking or even as much as a month of research.

Finding the hero Swordbird had been like this: When I was eleven years old, I was spellbound by fantasy stories, but in all the fantasy novels I'd read, none featured birds carrying swords (of course there were other animals carrying weapons). So I began to tell stories to myself in which armed bird warriors challenged one another in the air. For days and days afterward, when I ventured into the forest, I seemed to see flashes of something bright in the birds' tiny claws. *My eyes are surely playing tricks on me!* I thought. One afternoon, after I came back from my forest walk, I picked up a pencil and drew the profile of a dove raising a broadsword. In no time I tacked it onto the ceiling so I could look at it as I lay in bed. That night I had a dream about cardinals and blue jays that were fighting. From the dream grew the first book I know of with weapon-waving birds! Because it was a first, I just couldn't wait to write all about it.

For *Sword Quest*, it was even harder to find something really special to write about. Since Swordbird and Winger were mentioned in the first book, what could be new? After racking my brain for a long time, I had an idea: *Sword Quest* would trace back to ancient times. Who were the ancestors of birds? Some sort of dinosaur? But since that hasn't been proven, and since dinosaurs are so familiar, I didn't feel that writing about dinosaurs would be exciting at all.

One evening, I was flipping the pages of an ornithology book when a picture of an archaeopteryx caught my eye. *Here I am!* he seemed to grin. He had teeth, and claws on his wings! Birds with teeth—all of a sudden a door opened and I saw the opportunity of writing about chattering teeth, toothaches, and chewing!

I dashed to the local library to see whether there were any children's novels that had archaeopteryxes as characters, and there weren't. "So the archaeopteryxes win the audition for the bad guys," I said. *Sword Quest* could be the first children's book to have archaeopteryxes as its major characters. Cool! I guess you could say this is a secret of my writing—making the most of discoveries.

Nancy Yi Fan on Fate

YIN SOUL IS one of the main antagonists in *Sword Quest*. Because Yin Soul swallows a tear of the Great Spirit by accident, he becomes a half ghost. He searches the minds of dying birds and tries to trick them so he can come back to the mortal world in his victim's body by Hero's Day. This was inspired by one of the ghost stories my grandmother used to tell me. "In the crossroads, ghosts would lurk around," she said. "There they were, waiting to seize someone who was rushing by so they could use his body to return to the living world." I was only a preschooler then. I was so scared that once, in the fall, when I saw fog clinging over an intersection, I nearly flew back and avoided the place for days. Even now I can't forget the creepy story.

In one of the scenes in *Sword Quest*, an old bird uses sticks and the Yin and Yang symbol to tell fortunes. The symbol seemed so mysterious to me that when I was small, I used to draw a huge Yin and Yang on the dirt with my toe, and fill the black parts with buckets of water and the white parts with sand from the sandbox. I believed the Yin and Yang symbols contained the secret of the cosmos. So in *Sword Quest*, I added a fortune-teller to show Winger and Fleydur the way to the Island of Paradise.

Even today fortune-telling exists everywhere in the world because no one knows what will happen tomorrow and people like to know what the future may hold for them. Since what lies ahead is so unpredictable, many of us believe in fatalism.

In my second book, I dedicate *Sword Quest* to all who want to be masters of fate. It may seem as if it is too early for kids to think about fate, but we do think about it. I think from ancient times to the present, kids are always wondering "What shall I be?"

I seriously thought about fate when I was in my last year of middle school, and everyone was saying goodbye and asking, "What will you do?" I again thought about it when journalists interviewed me and asked what profession I would choose in the future. This is a big question. No one's quite sure about the answer, but we do have goals.

In *Sword Quest*, I let Winger speak for me:

"Fate is wind, not a river.
The directions of wind can always change,

EXTRAS

But rivers shall flow the same.
No matter which way the wind shall blow,
Dare to use your wings."

We can use our wings to change our fate and strive for a better tomorrow. If we take action instead of idling, if we put in a little more effort, anything can happen.

A Typical Weekend for Nancy Yi Fan

1. Do homework, of course—I have to keep up my grades!
2. Go to the library. The minimum number of books I check out at once is five. I like to choose my books as if I'm selecting courses in a well-rounded meal:
   - Soup—this is my nonfiction course. I usually choose historical fiction.
   - Main course—these are the books I like best, like fantasy. I usually get two helpings of these.
   - Spice—this is a book from a different genre than what I would usually read. I like to expand my horizons.
   - Vegetable—I try to digest one old classic and see what made it last.
   - Dessert—and for the cherry on top, I like to choose a book that is popular.
3. Start reading one of the books right away!
4. Go to a forest or a prairie to bird-watch, search for *lingzhi* (mythical medicinal fungi), and read under a tree.
5. Watch documentaries on the Discovery and History

EXTRAS

channels. Sometimes I can get good ideas from these shows for my writing.

6. Play with my pet lovebirds. They love to eat apples and chew on wood and paper. They're the world's most efficient living paper-shredders.

7. When the sun starts to set, it's time for some serious writing!

8. After an hour or two, my fingers become very limber, but my neck starts to stiffen. So after I finish my writing for the day, I polish my sword.

9. Go through my martial arts routine. I like to practice on the lawn under the light of the moon.

10. Sleep—and dream of books and writing.

Nancy's Top Ten Favorite Birds

1. Swordbird—He is the bird of my heart and imagination, and my favorite because he's the archetypical bird.

2. Northern Cardinal—I think the simple beauty of a cardinal in a field of snow is unsurpassed. It is a flame in the wintertime, and in the summer it cools the day with its watery whistling song.

3. Blue Jay—These lovely birds are bold and quite intelligent.

4. American Robin—A pair of robins nested near my window while I was writing *Swordbird*. Watching parent birds teach their young the art of worm-hunting is so fascinating.

5. Red-bellied Woodpecker—There are three known resident woodpeckers living around my home. I once found a tail feather of the red-bellied woodpecker while I was hiking.

6. Hill Myna—Hill mynas are experts at mimicking speech; they have a wide range of song from ear-splitting whistles to chirps. They're also very hearty eaters. I kept one as a pet for two years.

EXTRAS

7. Golden Eagle—One of the most widespread "booted eagles," found in North America as well as Eurasia, this bird has a beautiful golden blaze of feathers on the nape of its neck.

8. Northern Mockingbird—Though the mockingbird is plain gray, I very much admire its varied repertoire of songs and the bold aggression this little bird shows while attacking a crow or hawk.

9. Toco Toucan—The astonishingly large bill of the toucan looks very heavy, but it is actually hollow. I'll never forget the time when I saw one tossing berries in the air and catching them in its beak.

10. Great Blue Heron—I love watching these birds as they silently wade and stalk for fish. The most interesting part is when the heron catches its prey and swallows it, you can see a big bulge traveling slowly down the heron's very long, very slender neck.